That Girl: The Beginning of Betrayal

Written By: Tyra Racquel

D1446163

That Girl: The Beginning of Betrayal

Copyright © 2016 by Tyra Racquel

Published by Grand Penz Publication

Text Shan to 22828 to stay up to date with new releases, sneak peeks, contest, and more…

Check your spam if you don't receive an email thanking you for signing up.

Prologue

    I woke up to feel his hand around my neck, slightly choking me, and his other hand traveling down to my prized possession. I tried to scream, but he gave me this look telling me that if I was to even make a sound that I was going to die for my actions. I closed my eyes and counted to three hoping that my mother would feel that on the side of her was a cold spot in the bed. Can you just imagine waking up every night feeling unknown hands wandering all over your body? I wake up every night to see my mom's boyfriend Tyrone's ashy, black face staring back at me. Ever since the first day I met him, he has gave me this look like he wanted to take my soul and keep it.

    My mother's name is Robin Walker and ever since my father got locked up for LIFE for selling drugs she has been walking around looking like a lost puppy. All of the money my father had saved up and bank accounts he opened got seized when they searched our old house so my mom had to get a job and make ends meet by any means possible. We were not struggling too badly, but we had to change the lifestyle we were used to living. She met Tyrone a year ago and I don't know what she sees in him. He's lanky, always ashy, teeth yellow like buttered popcorn, and black like midnight. He's always beating her ass too so again I ask myself, why is she still with him? Why does she always put him before her own child? Why does she love him more than she loves me? They say a mother's love is unconditional, but if you ask me that's pure bullshit.

    I felt a hard ass smack come to my face knocking me out of my daydream. I guess he got mad because I spaced out, but I taught myself how to do that so I wouldn't have to dwell on this torcher.

"You little bitch! One day I'm going to fuck your little virgin ass and that might be the day you'll die too." He spat out at me. I watched him as he walked out of my room just as quick as he came. I got up quietly making

my way to the bathroom to wash his slob off of my body. He always liked to give me head, but I've never gave him the impression that I wanted him to touch me. I scrubbed my skin so hard that it was becoming raw, but I wanted his smell off of me.

When I went back to my room, I locked my door and balled up under my cover hoping to get at least a little bit of sleep. I dozed off, but I woke up to loud banging and screams.

"I'm sorry, I'm sorry!!!" I heard my mother scream for her life just like the other times before.

I tried telling her that just last week he came in my room trying to feel up on me and she didn't believe me. What kind of mother doesn't believe her daughter? A dumb ass one that's who. Sorry to disrespect my mother, but when she didn't believe me I just knew she was stuck on stupid for this nigga.

Just as fast as I woke up, I hopped out of my twin size bed and ran to my mother's room to help fight this nigga off of her even though she wasn't trying to fight back. I tried getting the door open, but of course it was locked. With all the life I had in me I tried to budge it open with my small frame. After finally getting the door opened I just knew that I knocked my shoulder out of place. Pushing the pain to the back of my mind I see him standing over my mom, punching and kicking her body repeatedly like she stole something from him.

"Didn't I tell you to stop questioning me like I'm your fucking child?"

As soon as those words left his mouth, I jumped on his back like a bat from hell. He tried his best to get me off of his back and succeeded by throwing me into the wall. I gained the strength to get back up, picked up a lamp, and just started hitting him with it.

I have never seen that much blood in my life! I just started to think about all those times he came into my room and touched me. With every memory flashing through my mind, I just kept hitting him. I felt a pair of hands grasping me and telling me to stop. Just to stop and that everything was going to be okay. I looked down and seen that he wasn't breathing anymore. I wanted to touch him just to make sure that he was dead. I stared at him for the longest before I finally stretched my arm out just to touch him. I needed reassurance, I need this to be real. I don't care what happened to me I just didn't want this man to hurt me anymore. Just as I blinked, he grabbed my wrist and I screamed.....

I jumped out of my sleep sweating bullets and felt my heart beating out of my chest. It was all just a nightmare within a nightmare. This has got to be the worst one that I have had yet. Is this a sign or am I trippen'?

CHAPTER 1

Alecia

Oh shit! Let me not be rude and introduce myself. My name is Alecia Walker and I am 18 years old. I have dark skin, long natural black curly hair down to my shoulder blades, curves out the ass, and I only stand at 5'7. Yeah, you can say that I am every man's fantasy and every woman's envy. I'm not stuck up at all though. I will be the sweetest girl you will ever meet. Ambition is the definition of exactly what I am.

Other than my mom I don't have any other known family except for my uncle Bone, but he lived all the way in Cali and I barely talk to him for various reasons. My dad, Darren Walker also known as Big D, was a well-known king pin and he got locked up being sentenced to serve time for LIFE. He had half of New York on lockdown. My mom and dad never got divorced, but I guess after being alone for quite some time my mom found herself a boyfriend that I can't stand and can't be left alone with by myself. Don't ask me why, but I have a bad feeling about him.

Tyrone was the name of my mother's boyfriend. He was what you called a true asshole and I don't know what my mother seen in him. I use to always see him outside with the younger boys on our block trying to get with girls that are younger than me. He would say things like "I'm not your daddy, but that's what you can call me" and "I see how you licking on the lollipop come and lick on mine." I have never in my life been more disgusted by his actions and I got sick to my stomach when my mom introduced us. She even cooked full course meals for this nigga and he would be sitting at the end of the table like he was King Tut or something.

Anyways, I have two best friends and they are literally my only friends other than a couple of associates. Mya has been my friend since we were in diapers. She's what you would call a mixed mami. She is half black and mixed with a whole bunch of other shit. Her black hair is cut into a blunt bob below her collarbone. She has slanted hazel eyes, a slender pointy nose, and full, pink lips. She stands at 5'6 and she's slim thick. Also, she's 17 so she is the youngest of the trio.

Ja'Nia (ja-ny-uh) prefers that you call her Nia for short since people always mispronounce her name. She's 18 years old, dark skin like cocoa, and has a coke bottle shape that'll catch anybody's attention. When I say anybody's attention it might've caught yours by now. Anyways, she is a free spirit type of girl. She wears what she wants, does what she wants, and says what she wants.

We are like the 3 peas in a pod or that is what everybody else calls us. We are in the last few weeks of our senior year and we will be graduating with honors. Thank you Jesus! Who said pretty girls are dumb? We are some young boss chicks making our mark in the world and that's exactly what will happen soon.

Ja'Nia

I'm pretty sure my girl Alecia introduced me to y'all already, but I'd rather just introduce myself to y'all again. My name is Ja'Nia Carter, but just call me Nia so you won't fuck my name up. You know those real cool, laid back, weird hippie type of chicks that everybody wants to be like nowadays? I'm one of those. I don't play by anybody's rules, I break them.

My parents spoil me to death and I feel like that is where I get my attitude from. I get what I want, when I want it and if I don't get it at that moment then I promise you I will get it later. My mother is a surgeon so I barely see her and my dad is one of the top best lawyers in New York so with that being said I wonder when they had the time to even create me. I love them, but I rarely get to see them due to their jobs. No complaints though since I'm never broke and I can just do whatever the fuck I want to do since I really don't have anybody watching my every move.

I wouldn't say I'm the baddest of the bunch, but I'm pretty damn close to it. Don't get me wrong I love my girls to death, but I just feel like Alecia think she's Queen B just because she's still a virgin at 18 and I guess everybody at the school idolizes her. Between me and her I just don't understand why people don't like me more I mean I'm the one that lives in a nice ass townhouse and I just got the new 2015 all-white Jeep Wrangler courtesy of my parents.

Let's not forget about Mya. She thinks she's all that too just because she mixed, but I feel like if you're mixed I might as well call you a mutt. Nevertheless, they say if you can't beat them then join them. I'm not a hater trust me, I'm just telling y'all like it really is.

"Are you still throwing that pool party this weekend Nia?" Mya asked me snapping me out of my thoughts.

"Yes girl, you know I have to so I can get me a new nigga because the old one is boring me." I said flipping my braids over my shoulder.

"Good because I do not feel like being at home on a Friday night. I'm glad you're not throwing this party when it's hot as fuck outside or my hair would frizz up." Alecia said looking through her phone.

"You have to think smart, not hard. Plus everybody who is anybody will be there just wait and see." I stated.

"Oh forreal? Who?! Who?!" Both Alecia and Mya said excitedly.

"Y'all will just have to wait and see." I said smiling.

Mya

My name is Mya Maria Brown and I am probably the sweetest girl you'll ever meet other than Alecia. I'm also the shyest of the group, but don't let that shy shit fool you into thinking I'll let somebody run over me. I'm a movement by myself, but with my girls by my side we are a force when we are together. I swear Fab said it best with his tall fine ass. Anyways, I just live with my mom and she works as a nurse working a 12-hour shift at the hospital so when I come home she's usually sleep and before I leave to go out I let her know just so she won't worry. My dad was killed before I was born so the only memories I have of him are the ones that my mom tell me.

It was finally Friday night and I was ready for this pool party Nia was throwing. After this it will only be three weeks of school left and I was ready to graduate! What are my plans after I graduate? I have a couple of things up my sleeve now I just have to wait and see if they really play out.

"HELLOOOOOOOOO? MYA!" Nia said loudly in my ear on the phone.
"Yeah, my bad I was reading something. What did you say?" I asked.
"I said are you coming over to my house so we can all get dressed in one place. Alecia is already here and then I'm going to drive my car to the spot. You might as well sleep over here too." She said.
"That's cool with me, I'll be over there in about 20 minutes." I quickly said.
"Ok I'll see you in a few then mami." Nia said hanging up the phone.
I wonder who in the hell is about to be at this pool party since Nia act like she couldn't tell us. I'm surprised that she didn't say shit since she can't hold water even if it depended on her life, but that's just her as a person. I can say that she can throw some good ass parties and I have a feeling that some shit might pop off tonight so just in case let me be ready. Oh, I did mention that I am a rider right?

***

Mya arrived at Nia's house around six and the pool party was supposed to start at eight so the girls were right on schedule. Nia decided she wanted to be different and throw her party at this inside pool that she found instead of the neighborhood pool where all of the locals be at. The mission for tonight was to turn heads, break some necks, and just be a boss ass chick.
"What swimsuits did y'all bring?" Ja'Nia asked the girls.
"I bought this two piece olive green one and along with that I just have my Levi shorts and matching wedges since I won't be getting wet tonight." Mya said.
"You won't getting wet, but I surely will." Ja'Nia said laughing and then turned towards Alecia waiting for her response.
"Well y'all know I'm not balling out of control right now, but I got this one piece all black swimsuit with the back out from Forever21 and I'm wearing my long lace black kimono with my black furry slides I made." Alecia responded.
"Nothing wrong with that chicka, you know you always slay in your all black." Mya encouraged Alecia.

"Yeah, it's nothing wrong with that. You'll look cute like you always do. On the other hand I'm wearing my all white Gucci swimsuit I just bought earlier today." Nia said as she was pulling her swimsuit out to show the girls. "I just seen it on the rack and I had to have it! Since it has gold details I'm pulling up my braids tonight so my gold hoops can be seen and I'll just pair it with the matching white shorts and flip flops."

"I know what song you're going to request the DJ play tonight." Alecia said giggling.

"Bitch what?" Ja'Nia said.

"Watch that bitch word Nia, but that song that goes like *I just fucked your bitch in some Gucci flip flops.*"

"My bad girl and oh I know what song you're referring to, but instead I'll be *singing I just fucked your nigga in MY Gucci flip flops.*"

The girls burst out with laughter calling Ja'Nia crazy and silly. Little did they know that she wasn't joking and that she was dead ass serious. Ja'Nia did say that she gets whatever she wants and that means every nigga that she craves for she fucks. Plain and simple. They knew that their friend was a little out there, but you can't control anybody's action. Just from her saying some shit like that anything was bound to happen tonight.

They continued getting dressed and started to rush because Ja'Nia didn't want to be too late for her party seeing that she invited people from school and people from the hood. This will be the classiest hood event before the summer and next would be the basketball tournament that happens every year. Finally walking into the pool area it was so thick that Ja'Nia didn't remember inviting so many people, but once you tell one person word will spread around like a wild fire.

"Girls I'm about to go around and speak to everybody, I'll be right back." Ja'Nia said while walking off.

"Yo it's real thick in here Alecia! No wonder why she didn't want to tell us who was coming. Looks like you're being watched girl." Mya said smirking.

"What are you talking about?" Alecia asked with a confused looked on her face.

"Turn around and look!" Mya said softly.

When Alecia turned around she seen a pair of hazel eyes staring into her soul, but before she could really get a good look at whoever was looking at her this hood rat named Bianca jumped in the way of her vision.

"Hey Mya and Alecia." Bianca said with a smirk on her face.

"What's the reason for you speaking to us? Last time I checked we don't fuck with birds like you." Alecia said grilling the hell out of Bianca.

"Damn such harsh words boo. Are you still mad about that nigga Ant?" Bianca said in amusement.

"What the fu—"Alecia started to say, but Mya pulled her away before things could escalate.

"Chill out Ali. You don't need to give that bitch any attention." Mya said trying to calm Alecia down.

"Yo why the fuck would Ja'Nia would even invite her? Matter of fact where the fuck is Ja'Nia at?!" Alecia said spotting Nia on the other side of the pool in some nigga face. Without warning Alecia marched over to where Ja'Nia was with Mya hot on her tail and grabbed Nia by the arm pulling her off to the side for a second.

"What the fuck Alecia! Don't be grabbing me like you my nigga or something." Ja'Nia said heated as hell.

"Whatever. What I really want to know is why the hell you invited Bianca hoe ass here and didn't even tell me. I almost beat her ass a few minutes ago, but Mya pulled me away before I could even pinch the bitch." You could tell that Alecia was pissed off by the way she was shaking.

"Look I'm sorry, but you know that I had to invite her. She's my cousin and trust me I don't like her ass either. Just relax and I'll handle it." Ja'Nia reassured her and walked over to Bianca.

"Yeah you better handle it before I do." Alecia was now annoyed and no longer wanted to be at the pool party, but she sucked it up and partied the night away with Mya right by her side.

CHAPTER 2

Alecia

Three weeks had flown by and it was finally the day of graduation. Our outfits had to be all white so I picked up this all white lace dress that stopped at the knee and some white chunky platform heels. To complete my look I flat ironed my natural kinky curly hair to a silky texture and it rested on the middle of my back. They decided to line us up in alphabetical order by last names so I was all the way at the end. While I was sitting there waiting for my name to be called I was thinking about how much fun I would be having tonight. I really was just ready to walk up, get my diploma, and walk straight out of this bitch without throwing my cap up.

"Alecia Marie Walker", my principal finally called my name and I see that out of the corner of my eye that my mom was showing her ass low key being ghetto as hell.

"That's my baby, that's my baby ... yassss she betta!" she screamed embarrassing the hell out of me.

I loved her with all my heart though. She was always there for me before her boyfriend came into her life, but I'm glad she could take off of work so she wouldn't miss my big day. I honestly thought that she would choose to hang out with her boyfriend Tyrone on her off day, but this just so happens to be the first day she has proved me wrong in a long time.

I grabbed my diploma and took my seat waiting for this to finally be over so the girls and I can go out tonight to celebrate. Just as the last speech was said our graduation caps were thrown into the air and you could hear cheering from all around the stadium. Tonight is my night, tonight is our night. We made it, we finally made it! I was genuinely happy for my girls and I. You know tonight we have to shut some shit down and we came prepared. You would've swore we were Charlies Angels.

Tonight everybody was going to Club Dreams. This was one of the hottest clubs in the state of New York where anybody from anywhere would come and turn up. It had three different floors with purple and green neon light, a bar on each floor filled with the best liquor, and on the third floor it had this glass wall that nobody could see through. If your guess is as good as mine then I would think that it was the office.

Anyways, I'm excited to get dressed up tonight and celebrate so let me start getting ready.

I decided to throw on this all black, lace up bodysuit with black high waisted pants and some black chunky heels. I let my natural hair do its own thing just to add some edginess to my look and applied *Cyber* by *MAC* to my lips making sure that my wing eyeliner was done to perfection. Ja'Nia wore this two piece burgundy outfit with some black strappy heels, while putting her freshly done box braids into a bun on top of her head. Just to be simple yet cute, she put on some mascara and added clear lip gloss to her lips. Mya put on an all-white dress that was flowy with some gold heels because she said she was "feeling godly", wore her bob in some loose curls, and applied *Stone* by *MAC* onto her lips.

My girls and I were ready to show out tonight. We finally made to the club and was able to skip the line just because my girl Nia had some major connects. The bouncer was her cousin so there was no problem getting in and getting a V.I.P. wristband. As soon as we made it to our section, Bianca decided to waltz her ass towards our direction and pushed pass me like I was Casper the ghost. I swear I was tired of this hoe.

"You dumb b---"I started to say, but Mya cut me off.

"Nah, Alecia don't waste your time on her tonight. It's our time to celebrate, fuck her" Mya said.

"That hoe is going to make me take it there tonight, but I'll let it go for now." I said.

"You good?" Nia asked me.

"I'm good." I replied back to her, but I can still feel this bitch Bianca grilling me from the other side of the club.

Ever since the 9th grade she has always had a problem with me. It's like she was always trying to compete and in my mind I'm always thinking that there is no competition when it comes to me and her. She fucked my ex-boyfriend Ant and the only reason why he fucked her was because I'm still a virgin. I went to his house one day to surprise him and I walked into his room not realizing that I was going to be the one that was going to be surprised. This nigga was fucking this bitch bent over his dresser raw! I ran out of his house so fast and the only reason is because I didn't want to go to jail for murdering both of their asses. I'm over that situation though because he wasn't shit to begin with so why dwell on the past?

Bianca stood directly in front of the table staring at me.

"Bitch I heard you was talking shit about me so since I'm in front of ya face repeat that shit," she yelled over the music.

"Excuse you?" I said mugging the hell out of her.

"Bitch I sa—"Bianca got cut off by Mya before she could finish repeating herself.

Why was Mya trying to be captain save a hoe tonight?

Mya said looking at me, "Ali don't let her get you out of your zone tonight."

"Nah Mya don't try to save this bird. Obviously she don't wanna be saved and she wants my attention so let me spit a few words to her real quick."

Hopefully I won't be interrupted anymore. I thought to myself.

It didn't take me but a couple of seconds for me to respond after there was a small moment of silence.

"First of all, don't come over here thinking you running shit in this direction because you don't. You're irrelevant to my life so why would I fix my mouth to even mention your name? Who are you to talk about? Dismiss yourself from me and my girls section or you will continue to get embarrassed hoe."

Of course after I said that I was sitting there with the biggest smile on my face. Why did she decide to try me like I'm some scary bitch in the club? I'm not a fighter, but I'll beat a bitch up when it's necessary. I was starting to believe one day that she might even try to kill me.

Bianca started looking around noticing that everybody was looking at us. She even gave Nia a look, but Nia ignored basically telling her that water was thicker than blood without saying anything at all. Even the little crew she was with had their mouths wide open from my response. I just sipped my drink and watched her storm off pissed.

"Ha-ha I don't know why she wants to continue to pick with me." I said sipping my drink.

"You can handle yourself, that's why I didn't say anything. She might be my cousin, but she's a trifling ass female" Nia said laughing.

Mya mugged us. "I'm too cute to be fighting in the club tonight! I got on this all white. I'm not about to fuck it up just because some bitch wants to get buck tonight so let's just chill and enjoy the rest of this night."

Ja'Nia and I just simply agreed with Mya because she would literally give us a speech in the club and I know I wasn't up for that tonight. It's just time for us to chill, relax, maybe dance a little, and look cute.

***

I thought I heard screaming, but then again what if it was another dream? I decided to stay in the bed because I did go to sleep kind of late so maybe I was trippen'. A couple of seconds later I heard some glass break so I rushed out of my room and straight to my mom's room which was at the end of the hallway. My eyes bucked at the scene that I was looking at. She is beating her boyfriend's ass with a lamp and she won't stop hitting him.

"Fuck you bastard. Don't you ever put your hands on me or my daughter ever again!" She hit him again.

I froze when she mentioned me, but I had to get her to stop before she killed him. Maybe I was too late.

"Fuck you and that little bitch!" Tyrone yelled trying to get up from his attack.

"No fuck you!" and with that she struck him over the head again.

"Ma! Ma!" I keep calling her name, but it's like she was zoned out.

She won't stop. I finally grabbed her and I could see tears running down her face. Blood was splattered everywhere and I got nauseous from the sight of it.

"Ma stop it! Stop! He won't hurt us anymore I promise. He won't hurt us anymore, just please stop!" I screamed.

They had to have been arguing since I made it back in the house and I guess she was tired of him beating her ass. I turned my head to the left, looked out of the window, and seen those blue and red lights that I was too familiar with. I knew what time it was. The neighbors probably called the police after hearing the screaming and glass break through these thin ass apartment walls.

There was a knock at the front door and I went to open it since I didn't want them to break the door down from not getting a response. "We got a call about a commotion and a complaint about loud noises going on in this apartment. Is everything okay?"

I didn't know if I wanted to tell the truth or lie, but I chose to lie so my mom wouldn't get locked up and leave me.

"Sir that call was —"

"No it's okay baby," my mom grabbed my shoulders cutting me off. The officers could see her covered in blood.

"Ma'am is everything okay?" This short mixed officer asked my mom with a concerned look on her face.

"Officers back there in my room laying in his own blood is my EX-boyfriend Tyrone. I struck him repeatedly over the head with a lamp and this is his blood on me. He might be dead." She said calmly.

The whole time I'm looking at her crazy because she literally just stood here and snitched on herself. That's why she didn't even bother to look me in the eyes. At this point I really believed she was fucking crazy.

"Ma'am I'm going to need you to step back away from the door and put your hands up."

My mom put her hands up and I stepped back watching them put her in handcuffs. Another officer went back to her room and indeed announced that Tyrone was dead on the scene and that they needed back up and the coroner to get to my apartment building ASAP.

I didn't know what to do at that very moment so I cried at the thought of my mom getting locked up for protecting us. My mom was probably going away for life, but she was defending herself so they would let her go right? I want to know what made her snap like she did, but I can't think about that right now. I really don't know what to think. My mind is everywhere at this point and I was so confused. I'm hurt right now because without my mom what am I going to do? I watched as they took her out of our apartment and I immediately called Mya and Nia. This was going to be one long ass summer without both of my parents.

***

I heard a knock on the door and I told whoever it was to come in. I was staying in a guest room at Nia's house.

"Hey girl, how are you feeling?" Ja'Nia asked me.

"I'm feeling ok. I just can't believe how my life changed that quickly in the matter of a day. 24 hours. Graduation night was supposed to be a celebration, but instead it turned into a tragedy. I can't believe this shit!" I said.

"I don't really know what to say Ali..." She started to say, but I cut her off.

"Just imagine your life without both of your parents. I lost both of my parents to the system and you still have both of yours. Just be grateful that you have both of them in your life not running the streets." I was full of emotion, but I really didn't mean to take it out on her.

"Look it's going to be okay and I'm your best friend so you know that I'll be here for you know matter what. I'll give you some time to get your life together, but sooner or later we have to get you out of my house and get some fresh air ok boo?" Nia said sincerely.

"Thank you for letting me stay with you. I really appreciate it." I said as I gave her a hug.

"No problem." She said as she walked out of the room.

In reality I wasn't ok. I was broken into little pieces and I felt like I didn't know who I was anymore. I wanted to just wake up from this dream, but then I quickly realized it wasn't one. It was real, this was reality and now I don't have any one of my parents in my life. My dad is serving time in jail for life and my mom was now behind bars too. I felt so numb and lost. Now all I have are my two best friends.

I overheard the police say that my mom beat her now deceased boyfriend so bad that his skull was broken into multiple pieces. They said after the 7th time she hit him, he was already dead and I knew the reason why she didn't stop was because she wanted to make sure he wouldn't come back to hurt us anymore. It's like every day he used her as his punching bag. I don't know why she stayed with him or even allowed him to stay with us. I just wish I could wake up from this fucking nightmare!

Since I've been staying with Nia and her parents they were doing everything they could to make me feel comfortable. They welcomed me with opened arms and gave me a lot of different advice on ways to get through this tragedy. I just wanted to be home in my own room, in my own bed.

My apartment held so many memories and I just started to cry at the thought that I still have to figure out what I want to do about school in the fall. Would I even be going to school at all? Shit is about to be different now that I'm left out in this cold world on my own. I know I can't stay with Nia forever and I won't.

I can't deal with all of that right now though because I got shit that I need to handle. I just need to adjust myself to what my life is now and hold off on school. Ugh, I don't know what to do but I'll just pray that God guides me the right way and I pray that I don't get into any deep shit that I can't get out of. Just like always I speak way too soon.

***

Ja'Nia

I just know Alecia did not just try to give me a speech like I didn't know what the fuck I had in my household! *"Just be grateful that you have both of them in your life not running the streets"* I mocked her inside of my head. I am very grateful for my parents and everything that they have given me in my life. It's not my fault that her mom decided to marry one of the biggest kingpins and his ass got locked up. If you're in the game you have to know that if you fuck up you either end up in jail or end up dead. She better be grateful that he didn't end up dead. I don't mean to sound like a bitch, but I'm speaking the truth.

I felt sorry for my girl I truly did, but she was starting to get annoying to me. She has been moping around for weeks and I really want to know when she's just going to move on. She's acting like her ass can't go get on a bus to go visit her mom in prison. Yes, I said a bus because she damn sure don't have a car. Then on top of that my parents have been in her face more than they have been in mine. Like what the fuck I'm their only child and they're treating me like the step child at the moment. Whatever, I'll deal with it right now but sooner or later she gotta find somewhere else to stay because I won't be feeling this shit for too much longer.

CHAPTER 3

Alecia

Ja'Nia's family lived in a nice ass townhouse, but I'm just so surprised that it is so close to the hood. The closest thing from the hood that is in walking distance is the basketball court and today there was the annual basketball tournament. Different teams would play leading up to two final teams and at the end one team leaves with the trophy and a cash prize. Since I haven't really been out somewhere in a month that's where we planned on going later today.

I sat outside on the stoop typing away on my gold iPhone 5s waiting on Nia's slow ass. She was in the house touching up her make up just to bring her ass outside to sit on the stoop with me. She said she was trying to tease these niggas and just let a couple of them spend their little chump change on her. I just laughed at her crazy ass and walked out onto the stoop waiting for her and now it's been 20 minutes still waiting on her slow ass. Mya was supposed to be coming by too just so we could all be together.

Mya finally got to Nia's house just as Nia came out of the door. I'm not even going to lie my girls and I looked cute as hell just to go to the court today. Mya had on a blush colored crop top showing off her flat stomach, white shorts cuffed right below her ass, and some blush colored sandals with gold accessories. Her hair was flat ironed with a side bang that was flipped. Nia had on this royal blue short romper with the back out and she switched it up wearing silver accessories with it instead of gold and she had her braids in two huge space buns. I kept it simple of course with my signature all-black style. I had on an all-black crop top with the words "I Don't Care" written in white words, black high waist shorts, and some black slip on sandals with my black natural hair all over my head and simple clear lip gloss. We all sent each other a glance, complimented each other, and laughed while walking to the court.

It was a humid Friday around 4 in the afternoon and everybody was outside today. When I say everybody, I mean EVERYBODY. From little kids, corner boys, prostitutes … EVERYBODY. This is what a normal Friday looked like in Brooklyn. We ended up stopping at an ice cream cart and picked out what flavor ice cream we wanted. While Nia and Mya were looking at the choices of ice cream, I decided not to get any so I was looking around and just so happen to look to my right watching this all black BMW pull up to the parking lot outside of the court. This pair of hazel eyes were staring back at me and I couldn't break the stare for the life of me.

"Alecia! Alecia!" Nia and Mya continuously called my name and I snapped out of my trance.

"Yeah?" I said turning my head just for a split second before reverting my attention back to the BMW that was no longer there.

The girls were laughing at something and I finally caught up with them just as this guy named Kane came up to Mya trying to talk to her. She always turned niggas down when they tried to talk to her so I wonder was she even going to give him the time of day or dismiss him like she does on the regular.

Mya

"Let me talk to you for a minute, ma." Kane said.

I rolled my eyes because dudes always came up trying to spit game to me and think I will fall for the stupid shit. Nowadays these females are getting pregnant by these niggas and end up having shitty baby daddies. Kane was cute though. Scratch that Kane was more than cute, he was fine as hell. He looked like a chocolate God. He had on a red and white Jordan shirt, black Jordan basketball shorts slightly sagging, and Bred 11's. I've heard his name from around the way and I remember him being at the pool party a couple of months ago. I smirked a little bit, but followed him as he walked away and told Nia and Alecia that I would be back shortly.

"So wassup wit'chu ma?" Kane said.

"What are you talkin' about?" I said nonchalantly.

"I peeped you at the pool party a few months ago." He replied.

"But you didn't say anything to me. What you were admiring me from afar?" I asked smartly.

"Actually yeah ma, I was. I was admiring a masterpiece." He said as he licked his bottom lip. I couldn't help but to blush. He knew how to be smooth with his words.

"Before today you've barely said more than two words to me. So why now? Are you checkin' for me or something?" I said with a little bit of attitude.

Kane smirked at me and said, "Yeah I'm checkin' for you ma now so wassup?"

I couldn't do anything, but smile with all of my pearly white teeth showing. We continued to talk for a little bit and I gave him my number before walking back towards my girls. He either was going to use it or not so it was up to him to make another first move. Of course Nia and Alecia had a million questions for me, but they would have to wait until later for all of the juicy details.

***

Alecia

We continued on our journey to make it to the bleachers and that's when I saw those hazel eyes again. I realized that Kane was now on the other side of the court chopping it up with hazel eyes. I couldn't help but to stare at him. It's like he had me hypnotized and I didn't even know his name.... yet. He resembled the rapper named The Game. Yes, he was just that fine with the height of 6'6, skin tone like sun kissed caramel, a trimmed beard, and muscled tattooed arms. I started to wonder what he looked like underneath his all black outfit he had on. I laughed to myself because he slick matched my fly, but in a more expensive way.

Just as I was undressing him with my eyes, he caught me looking at him and he smirked. What's up with everybody smirking and shit? I didn't look away this time and he winked at me I guess trying to see how I would react. I just smiled and winked back at him. Now that caught him off guard, but he didn't let that show on his face. Just as he was about to walk over to me I seen him wince in pain. Not realizing what was going on around me I finally snapped back into reality. He was

holding onto to his shoulder and the next thing I know I hear gun shots all around the basketball court.
POW! POW! POW!

King

    I remember seeing this dark skin girl somewhere, but I just can't place her right now. She bad as hell though. I seen her when I pulled up to the court, but I didn't want my whip to be out in the open like that because some niggas might be looking for me. If many of you didn't know who I was by now my name is Malachi, but at this moment I would rather be called King. I resemble the rapper, The Game, and I am a king pin that runs half of New York. I'm originally from Queens, but I reside in Brooklyn where my moms and sister stay. I also have a younger brother named Sage and whenever you see me, you'll see Kane and Sage right beside me.

    Kane was heading back towards me, but I couldn't stop looking at her. I guess she felt me looking at her so I just decided to wink to see how she would react. She started to smile and I thought that she was going to start blushing, but she winked back at me. Damn, fuck it I'm about to go over and see wassup with her because I don't want to seem like the shy type of nigga.

    As I started walking I felt a burning sensation in my shoulder and gripped it. What the fuck was that? I thought. I snapped out of my thoughts and realized some niggas was shooting at me. I pulled my piece out and started bussin' back at whoever was bussin' at me. Kane, Sage, and the rest of the team started bussin' at them too making sure they had my back. Running to our cars we pulled off making sure we didn't leave anybody behind. A couple of my soldiers were hit, but I forgot that I got hit in the shoulder as I winced in pain.

    I looked around the court making sure the dark skin beauty wasn't anywhere laid out. It's not like I wanted her to stick around while there was a shootout, but I did want to get to know her. Maybe I'll bump into her again eventually, but until then I was going to go to my personal doctor to get my shoulder taken care of...

CHAPTER 4

Alecia

Did they really just have shootout at the court? I don't know why I'm surprised, but I've never actually been there when they started shooting. I'm still running back to Nia's house making sure they are behind me. I swear all of this running shows me that I have to get back in shape, but I ignored my hard breathing and continued to run until I made it to her stoop. Once we made it back to Nia's house we instantly blasted Mya with a million questions.

"What's his name?" Nia asked.

"What did he want? Girl did you give him your number?" I asked excitedly.

She literally had to tell us to shut the hell up so that we could hear the full story.

"So his name is Kane, he said he wanted me, and yes I gave him my number so can y'all back off now?!" Mya said laughing.

"Girl he is fine as hell! If you don't want him, then I'll take him! Y'all are going to be so cute together though," Nia said.

"Who said we were going to be together? We haven't even had a real conversation yet." Mya smirked ignoring the remark Nia made and of course I had to add my two cents.

"You know that's going to be your man girl I don't know why you frontin' right now."

My girl is in denial at the moment, but I won't push her on that subject. We just went in the house because there wasn't any other reason to be outside and Mya ended up staying the night with us so we had a sleepover. We just started having a regular girl's talk after dinner and Mya's cellphone started going off again.

"Let me see who's hitting my line this late", Mya said.

718-760-8806: *Aye ma, what's good?*
718-760-8806: *this is Kane btw so I don't need the "who is this" text*
Mya: *hey, yeah I was about to say that. What's up tho?*
"Y'all its Kane!!" May screamed just a little too loud. I knew she liked his ass.
Kane: *I was just tryin to see if you and ya girls wanted to be VIP in Club Diamonds 2nite w me and the crew*
Mya: *hold on let me see if my girls are down*
"Okay so he wants to if we want to be VIP tonight at Club Diamonds. We always talked about wanting to go there so don't y'all think this is our chance? Do y'all know what type of people be in there? Celebrities, ballers, everybody who is anybody! It's even better than Club Dreams! So do y'all want to go?!" Mya said all in one breath.
 "Yeah that's cool with me only because I feel like getting cute tonight," Nia said walking to her walk-in closet looking for an outfit.
I rolled my eyes and replied, "I guess I have no choice huh?"
I mean it's not like I didn't want to go out, but I just wanted to have a chill night with the girls. It's either all of us go or none so I'll take one for the team since her future boo did invite us.
"Aw I love you guys!" Mya hopped on us and then we started picking out what we wanted to wear.
Mya: *yeah we'll slide through for a lil bit*
Kane: *aight, what's your home girls names so I can put y'all on the list*
Mya: *Ja'Nia and Alecia*
Kane: *aight I gotcha ma, see ya later*

Nia and I packed our outfits up to go over to Mya's house so we could all get dressed over there. It took us at least 15 minutes to get to Mya's house because she didn't live that far from Nia. She lived in a pretty decent apartment building that had a security guard outside all the time. After we spoke to her mom, we finally made it up to her room and started doing our hygiene, hair, and make up.

Ja'Nia wanted to wear her braids in a super high bun tonight so I did that for her while Mya wand curled her hair. I decided to flat iron my hair silky straight so I could look a little exotic. Mya chose to wear a red strapless plunging v-shaped neckline Steve Madden dress that stopped right above her knees. She paired her dress with some red Steve Madden heels, simple gold accessories, and *Ruby Woo* by *MAC*. Nia picked out this milky white dress from Bebe that had her whole back out, white strappy heels, and just a natural make up look. Last, but not least I chose to wear all black like usual. I couldn't afford anything too expensive since I spent most of my money that I had saved up for my graduation outfit. I picked a strappy black top that was backless and a tight black skirt that hugged my curves with an identical design going down the sides. Of course I had my black chunky heels on and my *Cyber* by *MAC* lipstick came in handy for the night.

Satisfied by how we were stepping out tonight we walked outside trying to figure out whose car we would be riding in tonight. After deciding that Mia would be driving since she was dragging us out tonight she turned up the radio and headed towards Club Diamonds. As soon as we pulled up we walked straight to the front of the line hearing bitches saying slick shit and rolling their eyes. Already knowing that we didn't give a fuck we strutted straight to the bouncer, gave him our names, got our VIP wristbands, and we walked right in with no problems.

Mya spotted Kane from a distance, but decided that he would eventually notice her so they went straight to the dance floor. "Bounce" by Jacquees started playing and that was my favorite song out right now.

"Bounce Bounce Bounce Bounce
We did came a long way from smoking in your mama's crib
She questioning what you want with him
And you don't know, go with the flow
Can't lose control, let me go
Time for relations, I'd die for the sex
I just want to see you naked, put my hands 'round your neck..."

Before I knew it I was slowly swaying my hips to the beat. Ja'Nia and Mya started hyping my head up and next thing you know there was a small circle around me.

"Kill that shit girl!" I heard Nia say.

"That's my best friend! That's my best friend!" Mya yelled.

***

While they were dancing King aka "Hazel Eyes" and Kane spotted them out on the dancefloor.

"Damn shawty wasn't gonna come and speak to me?" Kane said.

"You know these females play hard to get, but who is lil ma right there with all that black on? I seen her at the pool party a couple of months ago and at the court earlier, but them niggas started shootin' and shit" King asked.

"My G that's one of shorty friends Alecia I believe her name is. You must want 'er?" this nigga gave King the side eye and smirked.

"Nigga mind ya business!" they laughed and dapped each other up leaving VIP. They made their way down to the dancefloor to make their presence known.

Alecia

Some nigga must have been bold enough to get behind me, but when I looked back I jumped a little realizing that it was those pair of hazel eyes I've been seeing for the past few months. I think my heart literally stopped on the dance floor, but I kept slowly winding my hips to the beat and I could feel him moving with me. Hood niggas dance? You learn something new every day. I looked up and seen Mya dancing with Kane and Nia dancing with their homeboy Sage.

Once the song was over we decided that we wanted to sit and look pretty for a little minute so everybody headed over to the VIP section and some light skin chick with honey blonde weave down to her ass grabbed onto Hazel Eyes arm. He was right behind me, but I kept walking because whatever he had going on didn't have shit to do with me.

"SO THIS IS THE REASON WHY YOU'RE NOT ANSWERING MY CALLS? IT'S BECAUSE OF THIS BLACK UGLY BITCH?!" the girl yelled.

"Aye watch back!" I heard hazel eyes say, but that still didn't stop me from saying shit to this bird.

I instantly turned around and calmly asked her "are you talking about me?"

Mya and Nia flanked my right and left side, but I had everything handled right now.

"YES BITCH I'M TALKING ABOUT YOU!" she yelled again.

"Bitch? I got your bitch aight. You fu—"Hazel Eyes stepped in and cut me off.

"Aye ma you gotta show her some respect. I don't fuck witcha and you was just a one nighter and somebody I hit up for head so get over it".

Whoever this girl was looked so heartbroken and she just stormed off with her home girls right behind her. I turned to Hazel Eyes and told him that I could've handled that myself, said thank you, and continued making my way to VIP. *Don't let these hoes get you out of your element tonight Ali. Just stay looking flawless tonight* I kept telling myself in my head.

King

"Damn all I get is a thank you?" I said aloud to myself.

"Man don't even sweat that. Eve was about to get her ass beat so you saved the day. Just go over there and introduce yaself and wait to see what happens next." Kane said trying to give a little advice.

"Look at you tryna hook ya boy up", I chuckled and made my way over to the dark skin beauty.

"What's good ma, I just want to apologize for that again. I didn't mean to ruin your night if I did and by the way my name is King." I held out my hand and she gladly accepted it.

"It's all good just control your pets next time and there won't be a problem. Is your real name King or does everybody call you that? My name is Alecia."

I smirked because I knew that my mouth was slick as hell, but I can see that she already has me beat. She probably think that I can't handle her, but in reality it's the other way around.

"Ha you funny ma, but I'll tell you my government name when we get to know each other better." I responded.

"Who said that I wanted to get to know you? You might not be my type." She said with a grin on her face.

"If I wasn't ya type then you would've told me to get out of ya face by now and seeing how you can't keep ya eyes off me ma lets me know that you feeling me. Am I right or am I wrong?"

I'm not a cocky nigga, but to tell you the truth I don't chase after females, but it's just something about this girl.

"You're right, but that's the only time you'll hear that from me." Alecia said.

"Yeah ma aight if that's what you think. So when are you gonna let a nigga take you out?"

Alecia started blushing, "what do you have in mind Mr. King?"

I like the sound of my street name coming from her.

"Hmm I got a few things in mind ma, but just give me ya number and I'll hit you up later on this week so I can take ya out" I said.

I didn't want to ask her what she wanted to eat because females can never make their minds up. Fuck around and die from starvation if you ask that one simple question. Nomore words were spoken between us and we enjoyed the rest of the night.

Eve

King really just stood there and dismissed me like that for some random bitch that I've never seen before. I don't understand. I told him that I loved him and this is the fucking things I get? *"Aye ma you gotta show her some respect. I don't fuck witcha and you was just a one nighter and somebody I hit up for head so get over it".* His voice just kept playing in my head over and over again. I just hate niggas that lie so you can just say that I hate that I love this nigga. He tried his hardest to forget that we met when I was just 16 and he was a corner boy. I remember the first time meeting him as if it was yesterday.

I was walking with my cousin Nikki and she had this huge crush on Kane. I mean I called it a crush, but they actually had a little fling going on. I wasn't focused on chasing these niggas like she was. Honestly I was focused on school and getting the fuck out of my mama's house because my older cousin acted like he couldn't keep his hands off of me. He told me that if I ever told anybody then he would slit my throat from ear to ear. Not knowing any better I kept it a secret and each night he would come into my room and ram his dick inside of me. I just didn't understand why this was happening to me, but while Nikki was talking to Kane I felt King burning his eyes into my skin. I've seen King around before multiple times just because my cousin fucks with Kane. King was two years old than me and he was known a little out through the streets.

"Aye lil mama what's ya name?" King said looking at me still.

"It's Eve." I simply said. I wasn't really in the mood for conversation.

"They call me King—"He started to say, but I stopped him before he could finish his sentence.

"I know who you are." I didn't mean to sound like a bitch, but like I said I didn't want to be bothered right now.

"You aight? Seem like something is bothering you ma." He said with a concerned look on his face.

"It's nothing you can help me with."

"You never know what I can do until you let me know what's up." King said smartly.

"Look if you're going to stand here and be a smart ass then I'll just leave and get out ya way." I said as I started to walk off, but I felt him pull me back.

"My bad ma. A nigga just trying to get to know you and I'm getting the cold shoulder."

I looked him trying to see if I could tell if he was trying to play me or not. I wasn't trying to be out here 16 and pregnant. I'm surprised I don't have a couSON by now because I honestly wouldn't know how to explain that shit at all.

"I don't even know you like that to be telling you my business." I said.

"You can get to know me just like I want to get to know you Eve." Shit. I liked the way my name sounded coming from him. I started feeling some type of way and then I gave in.

"Alright, if you're willing to listen then I'll tell you wassup, but I'm not talking about it here."

"Aight give me a second lil mama." King said as he walked away.

As he was talking to Kane my cousin walked over to me with this "Mhm bitch what you about to do" type of look. I just rolled my eyes and laughed at her ass.

"Bitchhhhhhh I see you over here cakin' with King cute ass." Nikki said loud as hell.

"Damn girl shut up! I'm just over here talking. Nothing more, nothing less." I said.

King started walking back towards us so I told Nikki to shut her mouth before she fucked up things for me.

"You ready to go ma?" King asked.

"Ummm sure." I said not really sure where we were going, but I knew he wasn't going to hurt me.

"King don't hurt me cousin! Bring her back in one piece." Nikki said while laughing, but she was dead ass serious. That girl did not play about me.

"I got her. You just worry about what you and Kane got going on." King said as he chuckled and got into his car.

After I got into his car he began driving with no destination in mind. I just sat there wondering why was I really in the car with King and if he really did want to get to know me. Hoes talk in the streets and I've heard his name quite a few times. I might as well shoot my shot and see if he'll be real with me.

"So King what do you really want with a girl like me?"

"What you mean? I want to get to know you... simple as that." He said.

"So that's really it? I just don't want to get played."

He looked over at me and just turned back looking at the road. I started to get worried because I might've fucked up my chances just that quick. I need to learn how to keep my damn mouth shut. We finally came to a stop at a park and just sat in the car in silence.

"Eve... don't overthink anything ma. I said I wanted to get to know you, don't worry about anybody else. If I wanted to just fuck you then I would've said that, but I see you got potential so I wanna try to kick it with ya. Just know I'm here when you need me."

I can tell that he meant that for the moment. After he said that I went on to tell him about my cousin and after I did he looked mad as hell. He told me that after today I didn't have to worry about him and that he'll handle it. That's also the day I started to fall in love with King just that quick.

Just thinking about the first day I met him and now to him saying fuck me really hurt my feelings, but I know he didn't mean it. We've been through too much and I know that I was never and have never been a one nighter. I was there through all the lies and cheating, but I never left because I gave King my heart and I guess he wanted to give it back. Matter of fact I don't think he never fully accepted it. That's too bad because he's in for a fucking nightmare. He's stuck with me for the next 18 years!

CHAPTER 5

King

"What the fuck do you mean you pregnant?!" This bitch really just blew my high. Here I am chilling with Kane smoking a blunt and next thing ya know Eve ass calling telling me she knocked up with my kid. I know the bitch lying cause I haven't fucked with her ass in about two months.

"Do I have to repeat myself Malachi? I'm pregnant and it's yours." Eve said smartly.

"Aye watch that shit and you lying. I ain't been up in you for almost two months."

"I've missed my period for the last two months so this baby is yours. Don't be trying to play me like I'm a hoe! I've been down for your ass since I was 16 and you treating me like shit for some random bitch."

It sounded like she was crying and she knows that I hated when she cried. I was a ruthless killer, but I still did have a heart. I remember the day I met Eve and that same day I murdered her cousin. I did have my eyes on lil mama, but people move on and I moved on. She just didn't get a fucking clue after she caught me plenty of different women, but I guess she might've fell in love with the dick. Yeah, I know I might sound like a true asshole right now, but I'm a man. I'm not dumb though so that's why I'm checkin' for Alecia cause she seem like she got a good head on her shoulders and that's what a nigga need right now.

"King!!!" Eve yelled snapping me out of my thoughts.

"Huh?"

"Did you hear what I said? I'm keeping this baby."

"Nah, take care of it." I said with no emotion.

"I'm not killing my—"

"I said take care of that shit. Matter of fact I'm picking you up tomorrow and we gone handle it cause I don't trust you."

"I FUCKING HATE YOU KING!!!!" Eve screamed into the phone and then hung up in my face. She'll be aight. I don't know why she's still trying to hold on to something that ended so long ago. Yeah, I lied like she hasn't been a part of my life but it's the end of the road and she needs to get that through her fucking skull.

"Aye you good?" Kane asked.

"Nah she just blew my high." I said while rubbing my hands over my face. "I gotta go handle that shit ASAP. I can't have no kids running around New York. My wifey will be the only one giving birth to my kids and that's on everything."

"I agree with ya on that, but damn bruh you don't think you went too hard on Eve?"

"Hell nah. She'll be aight. She just don't fucking listen and that's why I treat ha the way I do. If I never went up to her back in the day then I wouldn't have these problems now. I'll hit you up later though cuz I'm about to head out." I had to go and clear my mind. If it ain't one thing, it's another. Only difference is I can actually solve this problem.

Alecia

"I swear I don't know what to wear", I said to myself looking in the full length mirror.

Finally deciding on this nude color crop top, Levi jeans, and nude sandals I hopped in the shower scrubbing my skin with Mad About You body wash from *Bath & Body Works*. After getting out of the shower, I applied the matching lotion onto my smooth chocolate skin. I kept my hair straight and just put a perfect middle part in my head with the bangs flipped. As for the makeup I kept it simple with eyeliner, mascara, and lip gloss. I never really try to do too much and I feel like that's why females hate on me. I refuse to be like these birds and walk around with two different skin tones on my face and neck.

Anyways, once I gave myself an all over glance I smiled because I was ready just in time and King was just pulling up outside waiting on me. He actually got out of the car like a gentleman and opened my door for me looking like he just wanted to eat me up right on the hood of his car. In reality I really would let him give me head and not feel bad about it after. I mean what I look like turning down some head? It would be like a bird turning down some bread. Ha, I'm just saying.

He had on this navy blue Polo shirt with Levi jeans and a pair on J's. I could smell his Calvin Klein cologne as he closed my door. *Damn he is so fine!* I thought to myself. *Damn shorty sexy as fuck I might need to cuff her* King was thinking.

"So where are you taking me?" I asked not even giving King a glance.

"Ma sit back and just ride" King said as he winked at me.

"Whatever you say pa," I said giggling.

We were riding for about 45 minutes before we pulled up to the fair and I got so excited. I haven't been to the fair since I was little girl with both of my parents and it just brought back so many good memories.

"You must like rides? I see you cheesing like a little kid over there."

"Yes I do love rides actually, is that a problem?" I said eyeing him playfully.

"Nah it just shows me that you can have some fun." He said.

"Oh, I'm surprised you didn't have something smart to say."

"I mean I did, but I would rather just whoop ya ass in some games."

"Put some money where your mouth is!" I said knowing damn well I didn't have a lot of money to be betting, but this was too tempting to pass up. I just want to see if I can really beat his ass. I'm just a little competitive and I don't like losing so if I lose the first time I might just play him double or nothing. We'll see.

"Bet!" was the only word King said as we walked towards the games.

***

Almost 2 hours went by and we were tired as hell, but guess who won? I did and I beat his ass in just about every game we played.

"I told you to put your money where your mouth is so pay up." I said as I held my hand out smirking with my other hand on my hip.

King chuckled and then said," Aight ma here" handing me $1,000. I've had $1,000 before just not all at one time in a long time.

"So are you hungry?" He asked.

"Hell yeah a girl has to eat after those easy wins."

"Ha, you got jokes and I got a better one … dinner is on you." He said as he started laughing.

I know he's playing with me because he is the one that asked me out not the other way around.

"Nay playa … you asked me out so it's your treat." I didn't mean to sound like a brat, but that's how it came out.

King started laughing," I was joking ma. "It's nothing to me, you can have whatever you like."

At that very moment "Whatever You Like" by T.I. popped up in my head and I couldn't help but to smile.

"I'll just settle for a philly and fries tonight because you wore me out."

I can wear you out in another way too. King thought to himself. "Aight let's go get some food so I can take you home."

He ended up taking me to a wing spot and I didn't want the night to end so I told him we didn't have to take it to go. I ordered my philly, fully loaded, with my cheese fries and a sprite on the side. I took a seat while he ordered his food. I folded my arms and laid my head down resting my eyes for a little bit.

"Damn ma, I made you that tired?" He chuckled.

"No I was just thinking with my eyes closed thank you very much Mr. King." I said sounding like I was irritated, but I only sounded like this because I really was tired.

"My bad ma… don't hurt me." King said holding his hands up like he was defending himself.

"I'm sorry, I really am tired and I know this food is about to put me on my ass." I said putting my head back down.

"I got you. As soon as we're done eating we can leave and I'll drop you off at the crib."

"Thank you." I said sweetly.

"It's no problem… so what was on your mind?" He said. I could feel him burning a hole in the top of my head.

"Huh?"

"My mom always told me that if you could huh you can hear." He said smirking.

"Whatever" I laughed. "I was just thinking about how I enjoyed this date. Never knew a hood nigga could be so nice."

"So you think I'm a hood nigga?" He got a serious look on his face for a minute.

"I just assumed I didn't mean to—"he cut me off.

"When you assume, you make an ass out of yourself." He said smartly.

"Well before you rudely interrupted me I was just going to say that I didn't mean to offend you. I think you're a gentleman with some hood in you. So if I'm wrong tell me what's right."

He really had me up in this wing spot on rare form. I was really wide awake now since he just insisted on cutting my ass off and correcting me.

"Aight ma. I see you got a mouth on you, but I like that shit and just to get you right I'm not a hood nigga. I'm a street nigga and yes there is a difference. To answers those questions you got going in your head nah I'm not a corner boy. I'm more like a CEO, I run my own business. From laundry mats to grocery stores I invested my money into them. I'm even thinking about opening up my own club soon. So are there any more questions on your mind Ms. Lady?"

Hmph a man with a plan I thought to myself.

"How do you know if you can trust me with all of the information you've told me? I could be the police baby boy."

He started to speak, but it's like he stopped and thought about what I asked him.

"I would've been peeped if you were a pig or not. I got a lot of them on my payroll so since I know you're not one of them then yeah I can trust that you're not the type of person to run their mouth." King said all in one breath.

I smiled and said, "Yeah I don't open my mouth too much. Rule is to keep your eyes and ears open and keep your mouth closed."

"Who taught you that? Let me find out that you're a queen pin." He chuckled.

"I taught myself and I may or may not be, but I'm pretty sure if I have more questions I'll ask you baby boy. Now go and get my food please and thank you." I said smirking like usual.

He flashed his teeth. "You got it ma."

I didn't want the night to end, but we might end up seeing each other more soon.

Ja'Nia

"Shittttttttt! You like that shit daddy?" I moaned as I rode Sage. He was relieving all of the stress I had built up. I think that I was officially in love with dick. Sage and I have literally been fucking like rabbits. I'm surprised that I didn't end up pregnant, but I wouldn't be mad. Why be mad when I know my baby would be well taken care of? That's the problem with females nowadays getting pregnant by a nigga that doesn't have shit or a window to throw it out off. Sage had everything and more so he was my savior right now.

He flipped me over and I already knew what time it was. This nigga loved hittin' it from the back. He told me one time that my arch was deadly and that was the main reason he stayed strapped so he wouldn't plant his babies in me all the time. My thoughts were interrupted by the moan that escaped from my mouth.

"This my pussy right?" Sage said pounding into me viciously. It was the greatest pain I've ever had and it turned me on to the max, but all I could do was bite my bottom lip. I didn't want to be too loud, but nobody was here except me and him so why not scream out in pure ecstasy. He slapped my ass with full force when he didn't get an answer.

"This my pussy right Ja'Nia?" He asked me moving his hips in a circular motion.

"Yesss...ssss....ssss! Oh shit that's my spot!" I moaned out.

"You gone give my pussy away?" Sage asked sliding in and out of me slowly. I didn't like to be teased and he knew that shit.

"Stop teasing me Sage!" I said while trying to rock back on him, but he made sure that he was in full control.

"Answer my question and I'll give you what you want." He said pulling his dick out all the way to the tip and then gently stroking my insides. Damn this nigga knew how to get me. I couldn't hold out anymore and if I had to tell that nigga that I would build him a house from the ground up then I would.

"Noooooo! Noooo I won't give it away baby. It's yours until the world blows!"

I guess those were the magic words because he started to put some work in after that. He had me cumin' back to back literally. I had to tell him to stop because my legs wouldn't stop shaking. Shit! He really does have some great dick and now I see why Bianca was crazy over him back in the day. Yeah, my cousin had him first but I seen him before she did. She got fucked and fucked over, but it looks like I'm still getting fucked and I lucked up.

I heard him lightly snoring snuggled up behind me. This felt great and all, but I really wonder what if I was in Alecia's or Mya's place. I honestly have a thing for Kane and King, but I'm not about to tell my girls that just out of respect so I'll keep it to myself. I can just imagine Kane's chocolate ass fucking me bent over the kitchen counter and I can picture fucking King outside on the balcony. *Damn, I'm low key a hoe or maybe I'm just a sex addict* I thought to myself. You already know once I see something I like I go after it. No matter what the circumstances are. I know King, Kane, and Sage are all family but shit they are all so damn fine. It's going to be fun fucking each one of them too. Call me what you want, but I don't give a fuck. One down and two more to go.

CHAPTER 6

Alecia

I think I spoke too soon once again. It has been two weeks since the last time I heard from King. Two weeks and I knew I should have never went on a date with him. I really felt like he played me. I know we weren't together, but it was just something about him that I couldn't stop thinking about. He was real laid back, made me laugh, and just so damn fine.

To get my mind off of him the girls and I decided to go get our nails and toes done since we're stepping out tonight. It's this new club called Blaze opening tonight so I said why not make an appearance. It wasn't like I was doing anything else.

Every once in a while we get our nails done at this place called Purple nails. This is the place where they do nothing but run their mouths and I guess we just so happen to be in there on the right day. "Girl yes King was over my house the other night. I knew he would come back to me," this girl with some honey blonde hair down to her ass said. I swear I've seen her somewhere before, but I just can't put my finger on it.

"Girl did y'all fuck?" I'm assuming that this girl is her friend asked her.

"Na, he just wanted some head and every wish he wants I'll grant it."

I curled my lips up just at that thought of King and this unknown female. So the reason why he wasn't talking to me is because he was with this ratchet bird? Then on top of that she just bragging out in the open about it like that shit cute. I hate females like that. Everybody does not need to know your business, but get mad when people that you didn't tell finds out. That shit blows me every single time.

"Eve do you know who that girl is grilling you?" Eve's friend asked her. "Girl that's the hoe I was telling you about from the club about a month ago. I was about to beat her ass because she was all up on my man." She said and was bold enough to look directly at me.

"Honey if you got something to say you can speak your mind because King isn't here to save your ass this time." I swear I was tired of these ratchet females trying me.

"Bitch who the fuck are you talking to? You thought King wanted you huh? Too bad because he doesn't sweetie. Especially all the times he's been with me this last week. I'll always be his one and only from here on out so leave my nigga alone trick."

That was her very last time calling me a bitch. I don't take that word too lightly. Call me whatever you want, but definitely don't call me a bitch because last time I checked I'm not a female dog and you'll end up getting your ass beat just like she is about to.

Just as she finished her sentence I punched her straight in her mouth with my right hand. I took her nappy ass weave, wrapped it around my left hand, and started beating her ass. She tried to claw my eyes out, but that just made me go harder. Don't try to scratch my face up, fight me! At this point I know I just had to black out when I felt Nia and Mya pulling me up off of Eve.

"Next time keep that bitch word to yourself. I don't need King and I damn sure don't want his ass. Tell him I said hey though and to pay for your hospital bill hoe!" I spat my words at her so fast I don't even know if she heard anything I said.

I ended up giving her a black eye, broken nose, and busted lip. I didn't even get a chance to get my nails done so I just paid for my toes and whatever damages I made. She really had me fucked up like I was about to let her talk to me any kind of way. I wasn't mad about King at all because he's not my nigga. He missed out, but like Gucci Mane said "miss one, next 15 one coming" so tonight I'm going to step out of my comfort zone just a little bit and give a show tonight. Now we have to go to another nail salon to get our nails done and then on from there it's going to be time to show out!

***

Later on that night my girls had me looking like a million bucks literally. They made sure that I was standing out and had me looking like I could snatch somebody's nigga tonight. I mean I don't want them other niggas at all trust me, but that doesn't mean I won't have their attention for majority of the night. The girls picked out this green choker midi dress with some nude heels tonight. My hair was put into a neat bun on the top of my head and for the jewelry I had on a simple gold Michael Kors watch and matching earrings. Mya had on my favorite color which is black and Nia had on all nude. I swear my girls are so bad and ambitious. That's why we're not friends, but sisters and I'm glad that they're in my life.

After giving each other our once over glance like we always do we left out of Nia's house and headed for the club. I'm not sure who the owner of this new club is, but I heard that he is fine as hell. I might run into him and make him my nigga since the old one didn't want to act right. Oh yeah I forgot that he was never my nigga I'm trippen' hard.

We didn't have to wait in the line long because another one of Nia's cousins were one of the bouncers. I just don't understand how this girl always had all kinds of connects everywhere we went, but trust me I wasn't complaining at all.

On the inside of the club it had 5 floors, each with different music playing and their own bar. On the first two floors it was hip hop/r&b music, the third floor was reggae music, the fourth floor was pop music, and the last floor was just where the office was that had an overview of all parts of the club. I've never been to place like this before so whoever designed this did a damn good job.

Ja'Nia spotted Sage and Mya spotted Kane from afar and decided that they would go over to speak to them. Guess who was right beside Sage and Kane? King. He was grilling the hell out of me. I guess he thought I was about to come and speak to him, but he thought wrong. I headed in the opposite direction of them and sat at the bar. I wasn't old enough to buy my own drink yet so I settled for a Sprite.
"So you ain't gonna come speak to me ma?" this deep voice said in my ear.
I just knew in my heart that it was King, but instead of letting his smooth talking get into my head I just rolled my eyes not saying shit. You just

can't go weeks without talking to me and then when you see me you act like everything is ok and it's not.

"Now you just gonna ignore me? You mad at me ma? I know I haven't hit you up since our date, but I had some shit I had to handle." King said sternly.

I turned around to look him in his face just to see that he was serious. I was still mad that I had to fight one of his bitches earlier because of her slick ass mouth.

"King I see that you're serious so it's all good. Thanks for coming over here to tell me all of that, but I would like to get back to enjoying this music and my drink." I simply said and turned back around in my seat like he wasn't even there.

It was quiet so I turned back around to notice that he was back over on the other side of the club with Kane and Sage while Mya and Nia were heading towards me.

"Alecia did you really have to do him like?" Nia asked me.

"Nia what are you talking about? Yeah, he apologized for not talking to me for two weeks but did you forget that I fought his pet earlier today or did you forget that quickly?" I can't believe she really asked me that shit.

"Ain't no need to get loud with me so chill with all of that bullshit." Nia said, but that shit was going in one ear and out of the other.

"Yeah whatever." I spat rolling my eyes.

"Look Ali we understand that all of that happened, but y'all not together Alecia so you can't get mad at him for that shit him and that girl did. He's single and you are too so that means both of y'all can do whatever y'all want." Mia said.

You're right I am single and I can do whatever the hell I want I thought to myself.

"You're right Mya, thanks." Was all I said before I headed to the dance floor.

The song "Acquainted" by The Weeknd was playing and I slowly started winding my hips.

You got me touchin' on your body
You got me touchin' on your body
To say that we're in love is dangerous

But girl I'm so glad we're acquainted
I got you touchin' on your body
I got you touchin' on your body
I know I'd rather be complacent
But girl I'm so glad we're acquainted, we're acquainted

Somebody came up behind me and I thought that it was King, but to my surprise it wasn't. It was this fine chocolate man that looked like he might be my "next 15". He even resembled the rapper Nas. Biting my lips I kept winding my hips really showing my ass. Next thing you know I feel my arm being jerked and King looking pissed off.

"Aye man why the fuck you out here disrespecting me like this. Got this nigga dancing all on you and shit. Man come here we about to go talk." He yelled at me.

He then turned to the dude that I was dancing on and said calmly, "don't touch her nomo or that's going to be ya life man."

He literally dragged me to the fifth floor and gently pushed me in an office and locked the door behind him.

"What the hell is your problem King? Did you really have to drag me off of the dance floor like that and embarrass me? I'm not a fucking child!" I yelled at his stupid ass. He was acting like he was my father and I really didn't appreciate that shit. The only dad I got is sitting behind bars for life.

"Alecia imma need for you to lower your tone when speaking to me. You took your ass out there disrespecting me and shit in front of my boys in my own club!" King said still calm as ever.

Next thing you know I slapped the hell out of King. I don't who he thought he was talking to because I wasn't Eve or any of these other broads out here. Yeah, I heard when he said it was his club, but none of that mattered to me right now. My feelings were hurt and I was finally ready to admit that.

"Just like I can't talk to you any kind of way means the same thing for me. I fought that bitch Eve today because she was disrespecting me again and then to find out that the reason why you wasn't hitting me up is because you was with her was disrespectful. Two weeks I go without hearing from you and all along you was with her. Man gone with that bullshit you talking!" I said without letting a tear fall.

He just stared at me for the longest without saying a word.

"Ma … look I didn't even know any of that shit happened between y'all. A nigga was stressed and I needed it to be released. If I knew that this shit was gonna happen then I wouldn't have did it. I wouldn't hurt you at all Alecia." King said sincere as ever.

"Look I'm not your girl so you can do whatever you want, you just need to keep your pets on a leash and out of my face." I said. I'm not about to let this nigga get in that easy.

I walked around him and headed straight for the door. Next thing I know he grabbed onto my arm and pulled me back towards him. I couldn't look him in the eyes or I probably would've gave into whatever he did or said. I was craving him so bad in multiple ways, but I just didn't want him to hurt me.

"Alecia look at me," King said as he pulled my chin up so I was looking directly at him.

"You must be feeling me ma or you wouldn't be acting like this. I apologize. I genuinely mean that and I don't tell anybody that I'm sorry. I don't know what it is, but there is something about you that I like and I'm usually not the type of nigga to settle down. You different though and I want to see where life can take us if you give me another chance. Clean slate and all. I'll even forgive you for slapping the hell out of me a few minutes ago ma," he chuckled.

"King," I started off saying, "I don't know what to say honestly. We're not even together and too much shit has happened already. I feel like you're going to hurt me and I don't have time for any of that. I don't want us to get together and then you leave me. It's like everybody is always leaving me behind so I would rather you leave me alone."

With that being said he let me go and I walked out of his office. I didn't even dare to look back because he actually had the look of shock and sadness on his face. I found Nia and Mya telling them that I was ready to go. They said their goodbyes to Kane and Sage and we left the club as quickly as we came. This whole day was terrible and I just hope there were better days ahead of me.

Ja'Nia

Damn I don't know why that girl really went out there and embarrassed King like that. She was acting like she didn't have any home training. I mean I know her little feelings were hurt, but you ain't gotta show a nigga that he phased you and that exactly what the fuck her ass did. I don't know what type of shit Alecia was on, but if I had a nigga like King then he wouldn't even have to worry about me doing him like that. I mean I was fucking Sage at the moment, but he wasn't King. In my eyes he was just King's little brother and in order for you to be the head bitch you would need to be with the head nigga. I won't push my girl off her pedestal just yet, but if she keep fucking up I might just have to take her spot next to King.

King

I had to let her walk out of my office and give her some space. I fucked up big time and it's crazy because she's not even my girl yet. I get a whole different type of vibe from Alecia and I know that if she doesn't forgive a nigga then I might not find anybody else like her. Something just went off in my head and I didn't mean to yank her arm like that, but I just didn't like seeing her throw her ass on some over nigga in my shit. Matter of fact I need to find out who that nigga is just in case he ends up being an enemy. Anyways, I can't sit here and worry about this shit though so let me go back downstairs and make sure everything is running smoothly for the rest of the night. Whenever she's ready to talk to me she will cause trust me I ain't going anywhere.

CHAPTER 7

Alecia

It has been a month since that night at the club. I've just been moping around Nia's house thinking about my life and what has happened in these past few months. It is time for me to get out of their house and get my own apartment. I already have my own car which is a 2010 Nissan Altima in the color candy apple red and that's my baby. I've been saving up from my whack ass job at the mall and I know how to do hair so that has been my hustle until I decide what I want my career to be.

Mya and Nia have been going out every weekend with Kane and King's brother Sage. Yes, Sage is his little brother and I was shocked when Nia told me. They were feeling bad for me, but as long as my girls are happy then I'm happy too. I think about King every other night and I know he was serious about what he said. The words *"You different though and I want to see where life can take us if you give me another chance."* Replayed over and over in my head. It was time that I put my big girl panties on and go speak with King face to face.

Me: *Hey King, are you busy today? I want to talk to you.*
King: *Nah ma, I'm almost finished handling business right now.*
Me: *Alright meet at your club around 3?*
King: *Bet*

I was actually excited that he agreed to meet up. I really don't know what's going to happen, but this will determine what the next step is for us if there even is an us. It was now 1 in the afternoon so I had at least an hour and 30 minutes to get ready. Luckily I washed my ass last night so I walked to the bathroom to brush my teeth, wash my face, and apply some light weight make up for today. Simple, but cute is the motto for today. I then walked to my closet and decided on a plain white oversized t-shirt, some Levi shorts cuffed right below my ass, and some all-white Nike huaraches. I left my hair in its natural curly state, grabbed my MK purse, and headed out of the door making sure to lock the door with the key Nia's parents gave me.

I pulled up in front of Club Blaze and really took a good look at it. Like I said last time whoever designed this did a damn good job and they deserve all of this credit that I'm dishing out.

"You must really like what you see?" King said scaring the hell out of me.

"How did you know that I was out here?!" I looked at him suspiciously.

"I do have windows that I can look out of ma. I was just wondering what you was staring at so I had to come and see myself," he said smirking. He looked fine as always and he was matching me by coincidence. His white shirt looked soft like a big fluffy pillow. He had on Levi jeans and some white air force 1's. *I need to stop playing and give him a chance* I thought as I bit my lip.

"Damn ma are you just going to stand there and undress me with your eyes or are you gonna come in and talk to me?" he said smirking yet again.

I rolled my eyes and giggled. He caught me red handed and I'm not embarrassed at all because I'm comfortable around him.

"Yes little boy, we can go inside and talk."

"Ain't no little boy here unless that's what you're use to? If so then you shouldn't be here right now because you're dealing with a grown ass man."

I rolled my eyes yet again and replied," look can we just go inside and talk."

He nodded and we made our way up to his office. I didn't get to look around last time since I was being dragged in here, but his office was decked out in white and gold. I just had to ask who designed this place because it was gorgeous.

"King who designed your club and office? Everything is beautiful in here." I said still looking around.

"My mother and sister designed it for me, but we can talk about that later. Now wassup?" he said looking at me.

"Well it's been a month since we last talked and I've just been thinking about everything that you said. I want to see where life takes us too if you still want me that is. I don't know if you have already moved on from me in this past month, but it's just something about you. You make me laugh, you listen to me, and I don't know I just get this vibe from you that I don't want to let go of." I meant all of this from the bottom of my heart. This man hasn't even kissed me yet and here I am expressing all of these feelings to him.

"Damn ma if I knew that you felt like that then I would've talked to you sooner instead of giving you space. You already know how I feel so it's no need to repeat it. I haven't moved on because all these other hoes want is my money, but I see that you just want my time. So yeah I still want your fine chocolate ass." He said with the biggest smile on his face. I jumped on him from the happiness I felt running through my body. Those are the exact words I wanted to hear from this man that I could finally call mine.

"By the way my government name is Malachi Grant."

At this point I knew everything was real. With that being said I gave him the biggest and longest kiss that I could muster up. Just feeling his lips on mine was everything that I could imagine. He then picked me up completely, never breaking the kiss, and put me on top of his desk. He made sure he had a good grip on my ass and squeezed it firmly. You could feel the sexual tension building up between us. He went from my lips to my neck and started to unbutton my shorts. He opened my legs wider while sucking on my neck still and his hands made his way inside of my Victoria's Secret underwear. I felt his thumb slightly graze my clit and that made my let out a moan. *Wait? What the hell am I doing? I can't let him get my goodies this easy. Should I stop him? Yeah I should.* I thought to myself.

I stopped him before things got out of control. Just that easily I was about to fuck him in his office, but I also stopped because I was still a virgin. Yes, at the age of 18 I still had my virginity and to me that was a blessing because I wasn't ready to be a mother at a young age. That's what they made condoms and birth control for, but I still didn't want to risk the chance. I also didn't want a fuck nigga to pop my cherry and for that reason that's why I always got cheated on.

"King, I have to tell you something." I started to say.

"We ain't even been together for ten minutes and it's something already ma?"

"If you just shut up and listen then you would know what it is already." I was getting annoyed.

"Aight go ahead."

"Okay… I don't know how you'll feel about this, but I'm a virgin." I said looking directly at him just to see his reaction.

"That's it? You had me thinking that you did some crazy shit or something," he busted out laughing, "ma that's aight it's not a big deal. I won't pressure you. I'll wait until you're ready. God really looking out for me to send me an angel like you."

At that moment I just smiled, thanked God, gave him another kiss, and he gave me a kiss on my forehead. Next thing you know he started tickling me.

"You gotta apologize for slapping the hell out of me ma … you heavy handed as fuck!"

"I'm sorry! I'm sorry! Stop before your staff thinks you're killing me!" I yelled loudly.

He stopped tickling me and whispered in my ear, "They can't hear anything that goes on in here because my office is soundproof."

After that he continued tickling me until we fell on the floor out of breath. He must've been reading my mind because the next words he said made me melt on the inside.

"You hungry babe?"

Those are the words that females love to hear and did he just call me babe? That's even better, but food is calling my name.

"Yes baby, I'm starving. I think I want some Mexican food." I said while tracing his jawbone with my index finger.

"I'm ya baby now? Ha, I like the sound of that, but aight let me go tell Kane to lock up when he leaves and we can be on our way."

I just rolled my eyes and chuckled. I can already tell Malachi aka my baby King is going to be a handful. I'll be his rider and I'll always hold him down no matter what. Now just because I'm saying no matter what doesn't mean I'm going to stick around for the dumb shit. I'm too smart and fine for that. I do not tolerate cheating or a man that put his hands on a woman. This is just the beginning of this long journey ahead of us and nobody will get in our way. King and Alecia is way better than Bonnie and Clyde in my eyes. Well it is for now.

CHAPTER 8

Kane

Knock! Knock! Knock!
"Hold up I'm coming!" I yelled.
Knock! Knock! Knock! Knock! Knock!
"I said I was coming!" I said as I snatched the door open. "Oh wassup Ja'Nia?"
"Hey Kane is Mya here?" Ja'Nia asked.
"Nah she's not here right now, but she should be back soon."
"Oh, well would it be ok if I stayed and waited for her? I just need to talk to her about something." Ja'Nia said.
"Yeah it's no problem. You know you're like family and you know that you're welcomed here." I said letting her into the house. She had this look in her eyes like she was up to something though.
"Thank you. I promise that I won't bother you or get in your way." Nia said smiling.
"Aight cool. I'll just be in my office. You know where everything is at so just make yourself at home. Mya knows you're over here waiting on her right?" I asked just to make sure I wasn't about to get into any shit.
"Yeah she's knows." She reassured me.
"Aight then." I said walking into my office so I could finish going over some paperwork for the club.

Ja'Nia

Not even ten minutes had went by and I could no longer fight the temptation. Yes, Kane was with Mya and I was indeed fucking Sage, but I couldn't help but to fantasize about Kane every now and then. I didn't know if it was his chocolate skin, pretty white teeth, or his demeanor that enticed me and I was willing to find out at this moment. Over these couple of months I have become obsessed with the idea of

Kane fucking the hell out of me so why not take this chance just to see what happens. Nobody has to know as long as we keep it a secret right? "Kane can you come here for a minute?" I said sweetly.

Why the fuck is she calling my name? Kane thought to himself. He still went to see what she wanted and sat down on the other end of the couch.

"Wassup with you and my best friend?" I asked him just to start a little bit of conversation.

"We good." Kane said. He didn't feel like there was a need to elaborate on that subject. "How are you and my cousin Sage?"

"I consider myself and your cousin separate individuals. We aren't together, but we have an understanding." I stated.

"Oh, is that right? So y'all just fucking?" Kane asked bluntly.

"Yeah we are just fucking to be honest, but at this very moment I don't want to fuck him anymore I want to fuck you."

Kane's smile left his face immediately. *What the fuck did she just say?* He thought.

"Huh?" He said.

"If you can huh you can hear. I said I want to fuck you Kane." I said smirking.

"Look ma" , Kane said getting up," I don't know if you hit your head on something, if you high on something, or if you just plain fucking crazy right now but that shit ain't gonna happen. I'm with your best friend. You just might need to leave."

What is his problem? I've never had a nigga turn me down before and like I said before if I want something then I'll get it by any means necessary.

"Kane I know you want me. I see the way you look at me. C'mon fuck me like you fuck Mya. I probably can suck your dick better than she can." I said biting my lips and I got up from the couch and walked up to Kane.

Kane pushed me back and replied," You gotta go ma. I'm not about to fuck up my relationship for some pussy that won't even be worth it."

"Just give me a kiss and it'll change your mind." I leaned in to kiss him, but the voice I heard made me freeze. I was caught like a deer in headlights.

"Bitch what the fuck are you doing?" Mya said calmly.

Alecia

"*I be representin', representin'... watch how I put it down ...*" I sang aloud while putting big wand curls in my hair. I fucked around and burnt my ear, but I wanted to look cute today for my man so I just put some grease on it and started back wanding my hair.

Today Malachi said that he wanted to take me to get some food, to the park, and shopping. I tried to tell him that he didn't need to spend any of his money on me, but he didn't listen to anything I said and just told me to be ready by 1 o'clock. We have been together officially for 2 months and it was now October so it was cold outside. I would say it was cold as hell, but just wait until next month comes and I'll be bringing out my fur coat.

Anyways, my birthday is next month on the 6th and I've been trying to think of what I wanted to do. I'll finally be 19 and even though that's not grown yet, I'm doing grown woman things. I still have the same car, but now I live by myself in my own apartment. From saving up money from my mall job, doing hair, and money that King has been giving me made this possible since I didn't blow it on material things. King helped me furnish some of it as an early birthday present. Of course I denied his help at first, but he insisted. I still said no, but he did it anyways.

When I moved out of Nia's house she was kind of acting funny, but maybe I was trippen'. I've been doing that a lot lately. She might be having problems with Sage or something, but the last thing she told me that they weren't together and they were just fucking. I told her that as long as she knows what she is doing then I support her.

Mya and Kane are some damn love birds! They are worse than King and I. I also found out that Kane is King's cousin. Isn't that ironic? Everybody is related. So that just makes it easier for me to triple date with everybody, I mean if you want to count Nia and Sage.

"Alecia!" I heard a deep voice from behind me scaring the hell out of me.

"Damn Malachi! You scared the hell out of me!" I said putting my hand over my heart.

I know he got inside of my apartment with the spare key I gave him, but he needs to learn how to make noise so he won't give me a heart attack and also so he won't get his ass punched.

"You the one that don't hear me callin' ya name ma. I've been calling your name for about five minutes and you in here day dreaming like a muthafucka." King said as he smacked me on the ass.

"Little boy don't do that shit no more!" I yelled at him with a sneer on my face.

His face changed from a smile to the most serious face I ever seen before and I kind of got scared just by looking at him through the mirror.

"Alecia don't fucking play with me. I'm not a little boy I'm a grown ass man so quit that shit. I told you about that shit the first time you said it."

"Alright, alright damn. Don't be a damn crybaby. Now give ma a kiss," I said puckering my lips.

"Nah you good."

"What you mean I'm good?" I said giving him the side eye.

"Just what it means. You good. You almost done getting ready? I'll be waiting in the car whenever you get done." With that said he really walked out the door and sat in the car waiting on me.

I can't believe he is really throwing a tantrum right now. I know he can't be serious. I finished getting dressed, making sure I locked my door, and got into his truck. I knew he was mad because he usually opens the door for me all the time, no matter what.

"Baby I'm sorry if I really did make you mad, but I was just playing." Yeah, I was apologizing.

He started cheesing big as hell and then to make matters worse he started laughing hard as hell.

"What's so funny?" Now I was the one that was big mad. So he really was just playing this whole time?

"Ma, I'm sorry but I just had to get you back. I done told you about calling me that and you continue to do so, so I had to teach you a little lesson about that shit. You still my sweet lady tho so it's all good."

"King fuck you. Now take me to get something to eat." I said with my arms folded over my chest.

He started chuckling," whenever you ready ma and what do you want me to e--, I mean what do you want to eat?"

Me. I thought inside of my head and obviously he was thinking it too with that remark that was about come out of his mouth.

"You already know what I'm craving so I don't know why you always ask."

"Ya you right I don't know why I ask you to pick the place because it's always the same one."

"But it's so good! You know you like the chips and the cheese dip. I can't make it like they do I always burn the damn cheese."

"Aight, just stop talking so much and we can make it to the restaurant so ya fat ass can eat."

Yeah I know my ass is fat and something else is fat too. I thought in my head yet again. I honestly don't know what's wrong with me, but my hormones have been raging lately. Maybe it's time to finally lose my virginity. I mean we have been together for 2 months, but it feels like it has longer than that and I feel myself falling for him.

I snapped out of my thoughts just as Kings cell phone started ringing back to back. He answered his phone without looking at the caller ID.

King: Speak

Kane: aye man I need you to pull up to my crib ASAP!

King: what's wrong Kane?

Kane: Mane--

glass shattering in the background

Kane: just pull up to the house mane!

King hung up his phone and told me that we had to make a pit stop before our date started. I was starving, but I didn't complain because I know that King will always take care of me.

We pulled up into Kane's driveway. I see Nia's white Lexus parked out and I just wonder what she was doing here. Next thing I hear is Mya screaming to the top of her lungs and that made me break out into a full sprint. No matter what I would always have her back. What I saw next just completely threw me off guard. Mya was on top of Nia punching her in the face and trying to bang her head up against the floor. I was in shock as I watched them tussle around Kane's living room. I just couldn't bring my feet to move. Why in the hell were my two best friends fighting?

"Fuck you stupid ass hoe, trying to fuck my boyfriend!" Mya said as she kneed Nia in the face.

I finally broke out of my trance and broke them up.

"Mya calm down and tell me what happened." I said to her, but she was spaced out.

I can tell that this was some serious shit because Mya completely blacked out and that meant something really did go down. Last time this happened she had caught her cousin and ex-boyfriend fucking.

"Mya!" I yelled and snapped my fingers in her face.

She finally snapped out of it and tried to go after Nia again, but I held her back from doing so.

"What happened?"

"I walked in here and she was trying to kiss on Kane and I saw him push her back, but she kept trying. She was really about to try to fuck him!" Mya yelled. I can tell she was about to get mad again.

I then turned to Nia and shook my head disappointed.

"What the hell were you thinking Ja'Nia? Mya is one of your best friends and you just really tried Kane like that. You do realize that you're fucking his cousin Sage!"

"Alecia shut the fuck up! You don't need to be talking about the shit because this doesn't have anything to do with you. Hell if it was up to me I probably would've fucked King by now, but you got him on a tight ass leash." Nia spat.

Hold up. I know she did not say what I think she did. I thought to myself.

"Excuse you what did you say?" I asked just to get confirmation.

"Bitch you heard exactly what I just said! There isn't a need to repeat myself." Nia yelled.

"Fuck you backstabbing hoe!" I screamed trying to get to her. King came out of nowhere, grabbed me by the waist, and started going in on her ass.

"Aye man watch ya mouth. I wouldn't even want ya if you was on a pineapple and water diet so stop that bullshit from coming out of ya mouth before I let my girl give you ya second ass whooping. "

Then I finally saw Kane. He was probably trying to break up the fight because his lip was busted. Mya always did have a mean right hook.

"Man you foul as fuck Nia," Kane started off saying," and don't think Sage doesn't know about this shit cause I just got off the phone with 'em."

"Get out my house bitch!" Mya screamed again trying to get to her again.

"Calm down baby, she's about to leave. She knows she's not welcomed here anymore." Kane said trying to soothe Mya.

"You were supposed to be my best friend! How could you do this to me? I haven't did shit to deserve this and you know how I feel about Kane. You're just like these other hoes! You're dead to me." Mya expressed with the coldest stare on her face.

"Fuck you and fuck you too Alecia! I don't need y'all and never did. Oh and don't worry I won't tell y'all secrets!" With that Ja'Nia walked out of the house and never looked back.

Mia and I looked at each other with a shocked expressions. *Secrets?*

CHAPTER 9

Alecia

Today was the day that I finally turned 19 years old. It has been a month since that bullshit with Nia has happened and nobody has heard from her. It's kind of like she fell off the face of the earth. I didn't even try to call her because what she did and said was trifling as hell. I don't know what's wrong with her and I really don't give a fuck what's wrong with her to be honest. I haven't even been by her house to speak to her parents only because I don't want to run into her and beat her ass. Yeah, I was still going to beat her ass for all of the slick shit she said. I wonder has she been plotting from the beginning on fucking our men.

Anyways, I looked at the clock and it was seven o'clock in the morning. Why was I up so early? At that moment all I could think about was the head King gave me. It was the best toe curling head I have ever received in life and it was so good that he sucked my soul out in the shower and on top of the kitchen counter. Even though he gave me head he knew I still wasn't ready to give my virginity up quite yet. He never pressured me or forced me to do anything that I didn't want to do and that's what I loved about him.

Yes, I love him and no I haven't told him yet. I mean we've only been together for 3 months and known each other for about 4. It may be too early and I hope it doesn't slip out at the wrong time. Tonight King is cooking my favorite meal which consists of baked chicken breast stuffed with peppers, yellow rice, green beans, and rolls with melted butter on top. My man was doing the damn thing going all out for me. I finally got out of the bed to get my day started and I spotted rose petals that made a way to the bathroom.
"Awww his big head ass is so sweet for this," I said aloud.
I picked up a note that he left on the sink that read:

"Your big head ass is finally up. I made breakfast for you downstairs. Pancakes, bacon, and eggs should keep you full until I take you to your favorite Mexican restaurant for lunch. Enjoy your meal and be ready by 10 so I can take you shopping."

- *Malachi*

I lightly jogged to the kitchen and picked up the silver platter that was sitting on my counter. On the side of my plate he had a glass of orange juice and red rose on the platter too. I swear he is just so sweet to me. After I got done stuffing my face I checked my phone and just as I thought my notifications were out of control. Twitter, Facebook, Instagram, text messages, and a couple of missed calls, but one stuck to me in particular. It was the name that read "Big D" meaning it one was from my dad. I know some of y'all might be thinking "I thought he was in jail" well he is and he has a cellphone that somebody snuck into jail for him. I called back immediately and anticipated on him answering.

Big D: *Hey baby girl! Happy birthday to my little angel.*

Me: *Dad ... I'm so surprised that you called me. I haven't heard from you in two years.*

Big D: *I know and I'm sorry about that. Some shit went down in the jailhouse and I had to cool out for a minute. I heard about what ya mama did too. I'm so sorry for leaving you out there by yourself.*

Me: *It's okay really I'm managing all by myself. I'm happy and I have a boyfriend.*

Big D: *Boyfriend? What boyfriend? What's his name?*

Me: *Chill out dad. His name is Malachi and he treats me right.*

Big D: *Aight now if I hear anything about this Malachi then he will get handled.*

Me: *Okay, I hear you. Now what's the real reason why I'm getting a call from you other than getting a happy birthday?*

Big D: *Alecia ... I might be getting out.*

I immediately dropped the phone. What does he mean he might be getting out? I swear he is supposed to be in jail for life and now he might be a free man again. Something doesn't seem right.

***

I was still bothered by my dad's call, but it was still my birthday and I had about two hours to get myself ready or King will probably be cussing me out. I walked in the closet trying to decide on what to wear. It's brick as hell outside so I know I need to dress warm and cute instead of just cute. I decided to wear this knee length tight black dress, black leather knee high boots, and this black and white mix fur coat. Happy with my outfit I quickly walked to the bathroom, turning the shower on while getting my shower gel out. I wanted to smell peachy today so I grabbed my goodies from Bath and Body Works hopping into the steaming hot water.

The water was feeling so good to my body before I realized that thirty minutes went by meaning I had only an hour left. I still had to do my hair and I decided to go light with the make up today. I dried my body off, making sure to apply my raw cocoa butter onto my dark skin. I unwrapped my silk press hair and attempted to touch it up so it could be flawless to perfection. Deciding to go with an Aaliyah vibe today I parted my hair so that the right side could be over my eye and tucked the other side behind my ear. I quickly applied my eyeliner, mascara, and lip gloss after slipping on my dress so I wouldn't ruin my makeup. Checking the time once again I had twenty minutes to spare so I quickly threw my shoes on and gave myself a once over look in the mirror. Happy with my appearance I grabbed my purse and jacket waiting to surprise King with me being ready on time for once.

Like clockwork he ended up calling me right at ten o'clock. I answered with the sweetest voice I could muster up.

"Hey baby, are you outside yet?"

"You must be ready ma? You sound eager as hell," he chuckled.

"Boy shut up. It's my birthday and I could be 20 minutes late if I wanted too." I said smartly.

"Yeah aight, only because it's your day...now bring ya ass outside before I drive off and leave you in the house all day with your smart ass mouth."

I rolled my eyes and hung the phone up on him. I refuse to start an argument with him on my birthday. I walked outside of the door and instantly started screaming. He got me an all-black Jeep Wrangler! It's decorated with a huge red bow on the hood. I can't believe he really bought me a car. My dream car at that! I ran to him jumping right into his arms, wrapping my legs around his body naturally.

"This is really for me? This is really mine?" I gave him a serious look.

"I told you I got you. Happy birthday baby girl. I love you."

Did this nigga just say that he loved me? ME! I thought to myself. I couldn't do anything but look at him. I looked into his eyes and saw that he meant every word he said and that he wanted to rock with me forever. I kissed him with so much passion. He accepted my kiss and accepted that I didn't say it back right then probably knowing that he shocked me. I was the first girl that he ever said 'I love you' too other than his mother and sister. I officially had his heart and not the other pieces of him females have had in the past. He just smiled and got in the passenger side of my jeep.

"Go head ma enjoy your gift."

He didn't have to tell me twice. After we went and ate at my favorite Mexican restaurant, we stopped by the mall. I wasn't really in the mood to just shop until I drop because honestly I just wanted to lay up with King and enjoy his company. He insisted that we go so I went just to make him happy. He knew that I didn't want to be there long so he pulled me along to the Cartier jewelry store. I instantly got excited. I spotted the rose gold and plain gold bracelets that I've been eyeing for a while. I turned around noticing that King had the bracelets in his hands holding them out to me.

"You're just full of surprises huh?"

"Anything for your big day ma."

I smiled showing all of my teeth and took the bracelets out of his hands. On the inside of the bracelets my name was engraved right along with his.

"A&M4EVA"

I loved both of the bracelets and I loved him so much I figured that it was the right time to say it back.

"I love you too Malachi, forever."

With that we kissed like the world was ending, but if it was I wanted to make sure that I was with him. Some say we are moving too fast, but I got him where I want him to be and he has me. None of that will ever change as long as I'm breathing.

From across the way we didn't see somebody was watching us, plotting. Shit was about to get deep.

King

This girl must have me sprung since I'm just dropping made cash on her. It's not a problem though because I know all the cash that I dropped on her will be replaced by tomorrow. She really must not know that she can have whatever she likes and I know that she doesn't like for me to spend money her, but I'm just trying to show her how she should be treated. I have one last surprise for her and then I would be satisfied for completing my task on making my girl happy for the day.
"Aight Ali, your nigga got one last surprise for you." I said.
"More surprises? Malachi what you've did already has been enough for me. You've literally out done yourself." She expressed.
"This is the last surprise ma I promise, but I need you to put this blind fold on for me." I said while pulling the black blind fold out.
"Nigga why in the hell do my eyes need to be covered? I know you're not trying to kidnap me!" She said laughing.
"Stop playing and come on. Ain't no need to kidnap you when you're going to come with me no matter where I go." I said confidently.
She rolled her eyes. "Whatever. Just hurry up and put the blind fold on me."
I put the blind fold on her and helped her into the car. Little did she know that she was about to meet my mother and sister.

***

My mother lived about forty five minutes from the mall and the whole way there Alecia wouldn't stop asking me questions. By the time she asked me if we were at our destination yet for the twentieth time we were pulling up into my mother's driveway. I can truly say that I was a mama's boy just because my father died when I was young, but until this day his name still holds weight. My father's name was Quinton Grant, but everybody knew him as Caesar. A true legend and I'm living up to his name.

Anyways, I finally got out of the car and went on the other side to open her door and help her out of the car without busting her ass. "Are you finally ready to know where we're at cry baby?" I asked teasing her.

"Yes big head and if we're not at a place with food then I'm letting you know right now that I'm going to be mad as hell." She said. I could tell that she was serious too by the tone in her voice, but I wasn't worried about that. My mom could seriously throw down in the kitchen. Tonight she was cooking her famous yams, fried chicken, macaroni and cheese with green beans on the side. Let's not forget about the cornbread!

"You ain't gotta worry about that." I said while taking her blind fold off. She started looking around and I know she didn't know where she was so got confused.

"Malachi where are we at?"

"We are at moms crib." I stated.

"Omg!!! Why didn't you tell me that we were coming? I don't even know if I dressed decent enough for me to meet her! What if she doesn't like me?" She started to pace back and forth.

"Calm down ma," I chuckled, "She'll like you trust me." I started walking towards the house and right before I could get to the door my mom opened it and gave me a big hug. It's been a minute since I've been out here, but I made it my business to call her every other day just so that she wouldn't worry about me.

"Dang ma, did you miss me?"

"Boy you know I missed you. You don't come see ya mama as often as you should." My mom said.

My mother's name is Ebony Grant and she stands at 5'5 so I really get my height from my father. With the money my dad left for us my mom found a way to make it work and when I got old enough I started providing for all of us. I just told her to keep that money for a rainy day just in case something happens to me or Sage.

"Malachi who is this beautiful young lady you brought with you tonight?" My mom asked.

"Mom this is my girlfriend Alecia and Alecia this is my mom." I introduced them.

"Baby you can call me Ms. Ebony." She said while giving Alecia a hug.

"Nice meeting you Ms. Ebony." I could tell that Alecia was nervous, but she'll break out of it soon.

"Y'all come on in standing outside like it's not cold as hell. Make sure to take your shoes off by the door and hang your coat up in the closet. Dinner will be ready in a couple of minutes." My mom said walking back into the kitchen.

"I have a feeling that she likes you." I said trying to make Alecia feel better and I kissed her on the cheek.

"You think so? She's really pretty. Where is your sister?" She asked.

"That girl probably staying over one of her friend's house so you'll meet her another time. C'mon let's go sit down at the table." I said guiding her to the dining room.

As I was walking in the dining room my mom was putting the food on the table. On top of the food that she already cooked she made a pound cake with her special frosting. She made sure that she made a dinner fit for a King tonight. We said grace and started digging into the food and my mom just came out of nowhere and started talking.

"So Alecia I want to let you know that I'm surprised he actually brought somebody to meet me. You're the first girl that he has ever introduced me to and I can see that you're making him happy."

Alecia looked surprised. Yeah, I never introduced a broad to my moms just because I knew that in the long run they wouldn't be in my life, but I had a feeling Alecia would be.

"I didn't know that Ms. Ebony, I'm just as surprised as you are and I want you to know that your son is making me happy too. I don't plan to go anywhere anytime soon." Alecia said looking me straight into my eyes.

Its official a nigga it really sprung and I pray that I don't do anything to fuck this up.

CHAPTER 10

Alecia

There was a knock at my front door and I knew that King was out working plus he had a key and Mya and Kane went on a little vacation so I wondered who it could be. I looked through the peep hole and couldn't believe my eyes. I opened the door and there stood my dad. This nigga was really out. Darren Walker stood at 6'3 resembling the actor Idris Elba. For him to just get out of jail he surely was dressed decent, but then again my father still did have a lot of power.
"Hey baby girl...surprise!" he said with the biggest smile on his face.

He was right I was surprised and caught off guard to see him at my front door. It hasn't been that long since he told me that he might be coming home and then on top of that he didn't even call me when he got out, but I guess a pop up visit is better than anything.
"Dad! You're really out. This must be a late birthday present for me huh? "
"Yeah something like that little angel. I just wanted you to know that I'm back and I'm better. I won't leave you out here by yourself anymore. Have you been up to the see your mom?" he asked concerned.
"To be honest no I haven't. The last time I seen her was the day she got sentenced. I don't want to see her like that and I don't think I can bring myself to do it." I looked down playing with my fingers.
"What did I tell you about not looking people in their eyes Alecia?" he said firmly.
"Not giving people eye contact shows them that you're not confident in whatever you say or what you might try to prove."
"Exactly so no matter what the situation is, always look people in their eyes. That's also how you can tell if somebody is lying to your or not. Now put on your coat, boots, and hat."
He was talking to me like I was a little ass kid I thought to myself.

With the most confusing look on my face I asked him, "Where are we going?"

His response was, "We're going to see your mother."

He didn't even give me a chance to protest. He gave me this look saying that I better not try to go against him and that I should put a pep in my step. Hurriedly I put my belongings on, grabbed my purse, and locked the door. Forgetting the keys to my car I was about to run back inside, but he grabbed my arm and pointed towards the black Cadillac truck we would be riding in. Okay, he was definitely coming back in style.

***

It took us a good 2 hours to get up to the shitty Whittfield Penitentiary. After going through multiple gates and getting past security, I was sitting at a round table with my father waiting on my mother. It's funny to me that this is the type of setting where all three of us will be together, but my family has been through a lot of shit to get us where we are today. Finally I see my mother coming out from behind this door that has a small glass window on it. Her long natural black curly hair was pulled back into a low ponytail and she was wearing an oversized green jumpsuit.

As soon as she seen me a huge smile spread across her face and I couldn't help but to run right into her arms and I started crying. I was crying so hard that I was shaking. I didn't realize how much I missed her and everything from that night came rushing back to me like a nightmare. *"Don't you ever put your hands on me or my daughter ever again!"* I just couldn't shake those words, but I finally let my mom go and that's when her eyes landed on my dad. She was just staring at him and a couple of minutes went by of pure silence.

"So mom, how have you been?" I started off since obviously nobody else decided to talk.

"I've been good Alecia. I'm holding up pretty well. What about you? I see you've gained some happy weight." She said eyeing me.

"Uh yeah I did. I actually have my own car, apartment, and I have a boyfriend."

"Oh so who is this mystery man?"

"His name is Malachi mom, but other people call him King. He makes me happy forreal and treats me how I'm supposed to be treated." I said cheesing big as hell.

I noticed out the side of my eye that once I said Malachi's street name my dad kind of froze up, but I think he realized that I caught him so he tried to shake it off.

"Robin."

"Darren."

"Nice to see you after all of these years. I see you landed yourself in a pretty fucked up place." He smirked.

"Darren you can get in the car you came in and drive straight to hell. Why did you even come if all you're going to do is insult me?"

"Just a little jail time humor, calm down and get those big ass jail panties out a wad."

I didn't try to laugh, but I couldn't help it. That last comment he made was really funny and I just knew he was trying to break the tension. My mom sat there mad, but then she started laughing too.

"Nah forreal though are you really okay in here? Do I need to put any money on your books? Anything you need just let me know because you do know we are still legally married." I swear my dad has the most serious look I ever seen on his face. I can still tell that he loves my mother, but she clearly moved on and her moving on caused her to kill her boyfriend and end up in prison.

"I'm good D, I promise. I'm so happy that y'all came up to see because I was starting to think nobody loved me anymore. Wait, when and how the hell did you get out of jail?"

Took you long enough to ask him mom I thought to myself.

"Don't worry about all that. Just know that I'm back and I'm handling business."

We already knew what that meant. Translation: Stop asking questions and mind your damn business!

"Mom I sorry that you started to think that I didn't love you anymore. I just really didn't want to see you like this. I didn't know how I would feel, but all I know is that at this time I know that I miss you so much and I wish that none of that ever happened. Even though I am happy with the way my life is right now, I know I'm not doing what I planned to do. I know things never go as planned though and everything happens for a certain reason. Just know that no matter what I will always love you and be here for you."

By the end of my mini speech my mother's face was drenched in tears. I was crying too, but I couldn't help it. Why couldn't Tyrone just up and leave my mother and me alone? None of this would've happened. I can't change the past, but I know for a fact that I can control the future. Before we knew it our time was up and it was time to say goodbye to my mom.

"See you later D. Make sure you taking care of our baby out there in this cold world while I'm in here."

"Man I got her. You just worry about being safe in here wifey. I'll make you straight and shit." My dad said winking at her.

Tell me why my mom started blushing and shit like a little school girl. I cleared my throat to make them realize that I was still standing there.

"Oh sorry baby, you know you're still my little girl no matter how much you grow up. Happy belated birthday and just know that I love you. Make sure Mr. Malachi is treating you right and I won't force you to come up here and visit me. You can just write me letters and make sure you stay in touch. Be safe out there Alecia and make sure you let no man stop your show," she said giving me a kiss on my cheek.

I started giggling, "Thanks for the miniature lecture mom. You still haven't changed. I love you too and I'll write you as much as possible." We watched as she was led back behind that door and I actually felt good about coming to see her even though I didn't plan to. I took one last look at the penitentiary and got back into the truck.

"I hope I didn't put too much on you for making you come up here," my dad said looking at me.

"Nah, I'm glad you brought me up here to see her because we both really needed this visit honestly. I love you Dad."

"I love you too little angel."

"Well since you love me so much can you take your little angel to her favorite restaurant?"

"Yeah I guess your old man can do that for your little greedy ass, but I have a question. When am I going to meet your infamous boyfriend Malachi? You know I need to approve of him before he gets too comfortable."

"Dad chill out. He's already comfortable with me, but you can meet him whenever you want to. Just let me know and we can set up a date."

"Aight I'll let it go for now, but I can't wait until I meet the little nigga that got my daughters head gone. Now let's go get some food."

I started cheesing like a little kid. Regardless he always spoils me and you know no matter my dad will always be my first love. He taught me everything that I needed to know to survive and now that he is back, I have my superhero back in my life. At this moment nothing can get better than this and I'm in a happy place in my life. Hopefully my life can stay like this for a good minute now and nothing will go wrong or did I just speak too soon once again?

***

Darren a.k.a. Big D

After I dropped Alecia off I decided to do some investigating. Yes, I have heard of this 'street legend' King before and I was just surprised that that is who my daughter was with. *How did she end up with that type of nigga?* I thought to myself. As a matter of fact I had to get clarification that this was indeed the King who owns half of New York. If it is then I had to make the ultimate decision on having beef with King because I'm trying to get all of New York back under my power now that I'm out. King was either going to give it to me with no problems or I was going to take it from him.

"Aye you got that info for me?" I said into the phone.

"Yeah! I've been hitting your line all day, but it's been going straight to voicemail. What the fuck is up with that?" the female voice said on the other end.

"Chill. I told you I had some business to handle today. I'm on my way to the house though and yo ass better be there since you're on my case."

"Yeah whatever just hurry up." She hung up in my face.

"This bitch mad disrespectful." I said to myself.

I met this bad ass female when I first got released from jail. She was the prettiest little chocolate woman I had ever laid my eyes on other than Alecia's mom. She was young, a freak in the bedroom, and had a smart ass mouth that I couldn't get enough of. In the back of my head I feel like I've met her before, but I keep brushing the feeling off. I pulled up to the house and seen her car in the driveway. *I told her ass about doing that bullshit. She must ain't learn nothing yet, but she's about to learn tonight.* I thought to myself.

"I see you brought your ass straight to the house." The anonymous female said smirking.

I grabbed her by the throat and held her up against the wall.

"You gonna stop trying me like I'm one of these young niggas out." I said.

"Ooooh daddy I like it when you're rough with me. Put a little more pressure on my neck!" She smiled in excitement.

"You really are crazy. You know that right?" I asked.

"I know you like that shit so don't try to act like you don't. Let me show you how much I appreciate you and respect you daddy."

I let her down already knowing what she was about to do. I knew how these young girls got down, but I ain't never met a freak like her. Anything I wanted to try, she would do it just for me. Needless to say, I was falling in love with the pussy. I started to get excited as she got on her knees, eye level with my third leg.

"I see somebody is happy to see me." She said licking her lips. I just smirked.

She took my member out of the boxers I had on and started stroking it in a slow motion. Looking into my eyes while stroking my dick she asked "how do you want it tonight daddy?"

"You already know how I like that shit."

With no further explanation she started to go to work. I liked my head sloppy and that is exactly how she was going to give it to me. She started with the head and licked around it just like she was licking a lollipop. Without warning she deep throated my dick and made my knees buckle. I tried my best not to nut so quickly. Making sure not to gag on my dick she relaxed her throat muscles and continued to give me the best mind blowing head I have ever received in my lifetime. By the time she was finished I was at a loss for words and get sleepier by the minute.

"C'mon daddy, I know I didn't make you tired. Come in the bedroom and fuck me." She said seductively.

Damn she knows how to turn a nigga on. I thought as my dick stood right back up at attention.

For the rest of the night we fucked for hours and fell asleep in each other's arms. I forgot about the information I asked about, but I'm going to make sure I ask her when I wake up in the morning.

King

Word around the street is that somebody is trying to take over New York completely. That's impossible because me and ole boy made an agreement and if he's trying to break that shit then he knows that he's starting a war that he won't win. A little birdy told me that this nigga name was Big B or Big C was trying to make that move though. Big worm, big perm hell I really didn't give a fuck. Niggas need to realize that they can't take over shit because it's my shit. I run this shit. Can't nobody fucking touch me. I have judges, attorneys, and even some pigs on my payroll so who the fuck is going to take me down? I'm the KING around this bitch. It seems like it's time for me to remind a couple of muthafuckas what time it is.

CHAPTER 11

Mya

I can't believe that I'm really here about to do this. I don't what I got myself into, but I know that this is going to be hard to get out of. I slowly walked up to the door and knocked on it three times.

"I'm coming!" I heard this deep voice say on the other side of the door. He opened the door and there stood Sage. He must've just gotten out of the shower because he didn't have anything on but some basketball shorts.

"Wassup Mya? C'mon in." He said.

"Hey Sage." I said walking in taking my coat off.

"What's going on... you good?" He asked me with a concerned look on his face.

"Yeah I'm good. Well, no I'm actually not. Sage I'm pregnant and the baby might be yours."

"Wait ma I don't think I heard you right. That night was a mistake and we promised that we wouldn't bring it up again." He said.

"I know, but I have to bring it up now since I don't know what to do." I said as tears started to fall.

"Ok, look we're going to figure something out ma. Just calm down."

He started rubbing my back and wiped some tears away from my face. He raised my chin up just so I would be looking him dead in the eyes. Out of nowhere we kissed and I didn't want to stop so I didn't. Right there in the living room we started taking off each other's clothes. He started sucking on my breast which were sensitive to the touch, but I was loving it. Without warning he entered my sweet spot and started fucking me with so much passion. I knew that I was fucking up again, but this shit felt so good. I was about to reach my climax and I could tell that he was reaching his too.

"Cum with me papi." I said with the slight accent I had. He granted my wish and let his seeds spill into my spot. We stayed in the position we were in before we caught our breath. Putting our clothes back on there was nothing but silence.

"Look I didn't mean for that to happen again, but I couldn't help it. I love you Mya and we'll figure this out just give me some time." Sage said to me with so much love in his eyes.

"I love you too Sage." I said giving him the biggest kiss. "I would stay, but you know that wouldn't be a good idea."

"Yeah its aight though let me walk you to the door."

"I'll text you later." I said before giving him a hug and one last kiss.

Ja'Nia

Unknown: Hey, I'm at my house. B is here so I figured that it would be a good time for you to come through.

Nia: alright, I'll be there in 5 minutes.

Don't think that I was just going to disappear and not pop back up soon. After my little run in with my ex best friends, I went home to see all of my shit sitting outside the front door. Yeah, Sage and I were living together but at that very moment I knew that it was over between us. I couldn't help but to think about what happened that night.

"So you really tried to fuck my cousin Ja'Nia?" Sage said not even giving me eye contact.

"It wasn't even like th—"

"Don't stand here in my face and fucking lie to me. As the shit was going on Kane hit my line and let me know what was up. So imma ask you again... did you try to fuck my cousin?"

"Sage...it wasn't supposed to go down that way!"

"Man get the fuck from in front of my door. You a fucking bird just like these other females! And to think that I was really about to cuff ya ass and make ya wifey, tuh." He chuckled.

"Please don't do this just let me explain." I pleaded. I was trying to think about what lie I could come up with, but he wasn't giving me enough time.

"Nah you good, ma. Don't call me, text me, none of that. We done before we even got started."

      With the last few words he said to me just kept replaying in my mind. *We done before we even got started.* My feelings were hurt, but now it's time for a little revenge. Yes, I'm the type of bitch that gets revenge. That day at the basketball court, King was supposed to be mine not Alecia's. She didn't deserve him and I know she still hasn't told him her secret yet and I'm pretty sure she's not going to. It would be so lovely if King was to find that little miss perfect – *HONK!!!* – I snapped out of my thought as I realized that the light turned green and I finally made it to my destination.

I parked my car, got out, and strutted to the door. *Knock, knock, knock!* "Who is it?" Unknown said. "It's me girl, open the door before I freeze my ass off!" I was literally shivering, but I was dressed for the weather.

      She opened the door and welcomed me into her home. I took a good look around and got a small peek of my surroundings before she tapped my shoulder interrupting my thoughts. I looked into the eyes of Eve and sitting on her couch watching TV was Bianca. You might be wondering how and why did I end up here, but it's time for payback. Yeah I did have beef with Bianca, but that was only because she had beef with Alecia. Now none of that shit means anything to me so it's time to put this shit into play.

"What's up cuz? I see you finally came out of hiding." Bianca snickered. "Bitch shut up. It's not like I went into hiding because I was scared to get my ass whooped so don't play with me unless you're playing with my pussy." I smirked and Bianca rolled her eyes. Of course she didn't have a comeback for that, but I didn't come here to argue with any bitch today. "Anyways, do any one of y'all have ideas for our revenge on Alecia or do I have to come up with everything?" I said.

"You act like you're the one she fought. That hoe put her hands on me so she deserves nothing, but the death penalty and before I kill her ass I'm gonna beat her ass for fucking with my man!" Eve raged.

"Ever since she embarrassed me at the club I wanted to kill her ass. Eve I know King is so called your man, but just to stab a knife through that bitch heart I might have to fuck him, suck him, or something and then record it and send it to her." Bianca said while smiling.

Before I knew it Eve jumped on Bianca and started beating her ass.

"Bitch!" *WHAP!* "You will not" *WHAP!* "Fuck OR suck my man" *WHAP!*

      I knew shit was about to get even more out of hand so I pulled Eve off of Bianca because I know Eve snuck her and Bianca wasn't down for that shit at all. She got herself together and tried to get her hands on Eve, but I had to step between this cat fight because we had shit to get done.

"Look bitches y'all need to stop all this damn back and forth bullshit! Instead of arguing and fighting with each other we need to be putting all of our energy towards killing this bitch. Eve you need to realize that King was never your nigga and you need to get out of your feelings. Bianca I actually agree with you and I feel like that's a good start on the plan." I stated.

Eve mugged the hell out of me and Bianca, but simply agreed with the suggestion that I made. She really didn't have a choice, but I'm glad that I didn't have to force her ass to do anything.

"So what about Mya?" Bianca asked.

"Don't worry about that hoe. She's only my concern, but since you're about that life B I might need you to do something for me."

"You think I can't do it for you Nia?" Eve asked.

"Either one of y'all can do it hell I really don't care, but I really want to start putting this shit into motion. So does anybody else have any ideas?" I asked and I knew that you could hear the irritation in my voice.

"Well we do need some guns, a location, and a plan B just in case some shit goes wrong but I'll get all of that handled." Bianca spit out quickly. After everything calmed down we sat down and talked about the rest of the plan making sure to go over everything without the bitching and complaining. By the time next summer rolled around hopefully Alecia Walker will be 6 feet under.

"Alright hoes I'm about to go. I'll see y'all later on this week. Just hit my line when y'all want to meet."

      With that being said I got up off of the couch and walked towards the front door making sure to have my hand on my piece just in case one of these bitches wanted to try me.

      Making it to my car without any problems I decided to drive by Sage's place just to see if he was home. I turned right on Wilburn Ave and made a left on Redstruck Street spotting his all white Bentley. I see an unfamiliar car parked right next to his. Not knowing whose car it was

I slowly pulled up and parked on the side street. Did I want to sit here to wait and see who comes out or should I just go and knock on his door? Seeing how I didn't want to cause a scene just in case another bitch was there I decided I'm going to stay in the car and turn my heat all the way up so I won't freeze to death. Feeling in my backseat for my thick blanket, gloves and an extra sweater to throw on I was about to get real comfortable.

About 30 minutes went by before I seen a small silhouette walking out of his house and he was standing at the front door watching this woman making sure she made it to her car. Wait a minute. Why does that woman resemble Mya so much? What the hell? That is Mya! Why is Mya at Sage's house so late at night? Maybe I can use this to my advantage. I quickly took out my phone and started snapping pictures of both of them.

After she drove off, I got out of the car and walked up to his door ringing the doorbell.

"Mya did you forget—," Sage was looking at me like he seen a ghost.

"Oh you thought I was Mya huh? Well I'm not. Hey baby I'm back!" I said trying to give him a kiss.

"Man why are you here Nia? You disappeared and it should've stayed like that to be honest."

"Stop all that damn cry baby bullshit. Are you going to let me in or not?" I gave the most innocent look that I could muster up.

He smacked his lips," come in Ja'Nia, but you're not staying here for a long."

"Ok daddy." I said snickering.

"So why are you really here? I told you to never come back and obviously you don't know how to listen."

"No the real question is why Mya was here?"

"You worried about the wrong thing."

"Nah actually I'm worried about the right thing, but I'll let it go for the time being. So you don't miss me at all baby?" I said walking up to him.

"You don't miss the way I rub your back, ride you, or deep throat that dick big daddy?"

"Aye man back up. I'm not about to do this with you ma. You fucked that up when you tried to fuck my fam."

"I'm sorry Sage. It wasn't suppose to go down like that. I told you that and you didn't believe me. Didn't even give me a chance to explain so let me do that now."

"Do it now then, explain?" he simply just stared at me.

I took that as my chance to get this nigga when he's weak so I got on my knees and started unbuckling his pants.

"What are you doing Nia? Get up ma this ain't about to happen."

"Shhh! Just let me take care of you Sage. I need you. My body craves for you. I love you Sage and I didn't mean to hurt you baby."

After I said that it's like his whole demeanor changed so I quickly took his beautiful caramel colored dick out of the polo boxers he was wearing and started to lick the tip teasing him. After seeing that he wasn't going to stop me I started licking up and down his shaft making sure to get it sloppy just like he likes it. Finally deciding not to tease him anymore I deep throated his whole 9 inches and that sent him into pure bliss. Making sure to hum while his dick was down my throat I started playing with his balls. I knew that that shit made him crazy and looking up I seen his eyes rolling into the back of his head. His legs started to slightly give out and without warning he came down my throat, but I gladly took all of his sweet sauce that he had to offer. He leaned up against the wall trying to catch his breath.

"Do you need some water or something?" I asked him.

All he could was shake his head so I headed to the kitchen and got a glass from the cabinet. I quickly peeked around the corner to make sure that he wasn't coming I took out 8 crushed up pills and put it in his water making sure to blend it so he wouldn't detect it. Walking swiftly out of the kitchen I made it back to him with a quickness and gave him his water. Without missing one beat he drunk the whole glass, sat it down, and walked towards me. I didn't know what to expect and I was really caught off guard when he came and crushed his lips onto mine.

"I love you too Nia. You know how to make a nigga weak." He said sincerely.

I just know he didn't just tell me that he loves me not knowing that in the matter of minutes he'll be dead.

"Come lay with me ma and we can talk about everything in the morning." He said groggily.

I didn't have a choice, but to accept his offer. I'm pissed that now he wants to admit to loving me after I poisoned him. *I did like him and we could've made something work out, but now it's too late. Oh well.* I thought to myself.

After laying down about an hour flew by and that's when I turned towards him realizing that he stopped breathing. Sage was dead and I didn't have any emotion for it. I hopped out of his bed and called my cousin that is always getting me into the clubs.

Ja'Nia: Hey Rick I need you to handle something for me.

Rick: No problem cuz, you know I got you.

Waiting for my cousin to arrive I looked back at the beautiful figure laying on the bed. He was really dead, but did I really have to give a fuck at this moment? No. Fuck him anyways. Yeah, he could've been my husband but I wanted King and been craving for him. One way or another he will be mine even if I have to kill his own flesh and blood.

CHAPTER 12

Alecia

"Sweetest thing I ever known was like a kiss on the collarbone" I was singing my heart out waiting for King to come over to my place. Just as I was thinking about him his name popped up on my phone with a text reading that he wouldn't be able to see me until later on tonight and that he has a surprise for me. I simply text okay baby and decided to hit up my best friend since we haven't hung out in a minute. I think we both need a girl's day to catch up on some shit so I dialed her number. It rung two times before she finally answered.

Mya: Heyyyyyyyy girl!

Me: Hey boo, I miss you so much!

Mya: I miss you too! What are you doing today? You want to go to the mall and have lunch?

Me: That's funny because that is why I was calling you. I wanted to spend time with my best friend.

Mya: Girl you know we think just alike, but I'm already dressed. Do you want me to come pick you up? I have some surprising news to tell you anyways.

Me: Damn everybody has surprises for me today huh? But yeah girl you can come pick me. All I have to do is freshen up and just let me know when you're outside.

Mya: Okay bestie, I'll see you in a minute.

Without responding back I just hung the phone up because I know Mya's ass drives like a bat out of hell. I went into my bathroom and reapplied some eyeliner and mascara just so it would be fresh. I threw on a thick olive green cardigan with a long sleeve white shirt underneath and some dark wash Levi jeans. I paired my outfit with some olive green Uggs and I made sure to grab my North face jacket and matching gloves. Yes, I was trying to be cute today not freezing my ass off. Just as I slipped my gloves on Mya told me that she was outside and I see that she made it to my place within 15 minutes so I know her ass was speeding over here.

I swiftly walked around my apartment making sure that I didn't leave anything behind that I might need. After making sure that my door was locked I lightly jogged to Mya's 2012 Silver Jeep so that she's been raving about for the longest. Kane wanted to buy her something nicer than this, but he didn't push the issue and she was happy with what she picked out. Both one of us was never the flashy type and I think that it was drawn us to King and Kane. I entered her car and she basically tackled me just because we haven't seen each other in a couple of weeks.

"Oh I swear I've missed you so much! We don't need to go that long without hanging with each other ever again." Mya said.

"I know I missed my mixed mami! So what is this surprise you have for me?" I asked giving her the side eye.

"It's a surprise for a reason Alecia. Stop being impatient okay? I'll tell you while we are eating lunch."

"Yeah okay. I can't wait until I find out because you got me getting anxious girl. So how are you and Kane?" I said changing the subject.

"We are good girl. He makes me so happy and I honestly can say that I'm falling for him." Mya started cheesing big as hell.

"Aw that's so sweet. I feel the same way about King. He's my heart girl. I literally was spoiled for my birthday with some new furniture, new car, and two Cartier bracelets that I've been dying to have. King out did himself honestly." I mumbled the last part.

"What's wrong boo? You feel like he's doing too much for you?" Mya asked concerned.

"Yes sometimes I do, but no matter what I know he's going to spoil me every chance he gets. I know if we were to ever have a child he would go overboard."

By the time I said my last sentence we pulled into the parking lot of Longhorn Steakhouse. I know y'all think oh finally she's not eating Mexican food. I can't help it that I like chicken quesadillas and their chips and cheese dip gives me my life every time I go. After being seated, we started looking over the menus and I think I wanted some wine to go with my meal today.

"Hello, my name is Sara and I'll be your waitress. We have many specials today so here's a menu just in case you want to try one today and if you're not ready to order then I can just take down what you ladies would like to drink."

"Thank you Sara. Well today I would just like some water with a lot of lemons. Also, I'm ready to order my food. I want the baby back ribs with a loaded baked potato and steamed broccoli on the side."

I'm surprised that Mya didn't want to drink today, but that wouldn't stop me from getting my drink on.

"Well I would like red wine and also a glass of water. I would also like the 9 oz. steak cooked well done with a loaded baked potato and fries on the side. Can we also get a basket of rolls with butter?" I liked potatoes too much, don't judge me.

"Yes ma'am," she repeated our order back to us," will that be all for you ladies today?"

"No we're fine so far." I responded.

"Okay I will put your orders in and I'll be back with your drinks."

"Thank you." Mya sweetly said. She loved when people didn't have attitudes while doing their jobs.

"So Alecia before I tell you what the surprise is I just want to tell you that I love you and I thank you for pushing me to actually talk to Kane that day at the basketball court. Because of you my life has changed and I am so happy with everything that is going on right now." Mya started off.

Before I could respond she pulled this yellow gift bag out of her purse and handed it to me.

"Girl what is this?" I asked looking at the bad suspiciously.

"Instead of looking at the bag like it has a disease, open it up crazy girl." She said giggling.

I opened the bag and what I seen instantly brought tears to my eyes. I'm going to be an auntie!

"Oh my god! You're pregnant?! Mya you're pregnant! Oh my god! Forreal! I'm going to be an auntie!" At this point tears were streaming down my face. I've never been so happy for her ever in my life. I remember when we were little and all we use to talk about is being in love and having families. They always said that I would be the first one, but instead Mya is. My best friend is having a baby.

"Ahhh how far along are you?"

"I'm not sure. I have a doctor's appointment later on this week and I wanted to know if you wanted to go with me?"

"Of course I want to go with you girl! This is exciting. Have you told Kane yet?"

"No."

"What in the hell do you mean no Mya?" looking at her like she was crazy.

"Like I said no because I wanted to see how far along I was first and surprise him with an ultrasound. Keep calm girl. He's going to find out trust hell he's the one that got me pregnant."

"Oh okay girl you had me worried for a little bit."

We both chuckled and soon after that our food was brought out. No more words were spoken as we devoured our food in about 20 minutes. Both of us were stuffed like ticks and didn't even finish all of our food. Not even wanting to go plates we got the check and left Sara a hefty tip on the table since she did a good ass job with serving us.

"Where to next trick?" I said lightly bumping Mya with my hip.

"To the mall to drop some bands bih!" Mya started twerking.

"Girl calm down. You're about to be a mother. You can't be out here acting like a hood rat."

Mya paused and looked at me like I was crazy. I just busted out laughing in her face.

"Yo you mad disrespectful. I should leave your ass so you can call King to come pick your ass up tramp."

"Don't be mad best friend be glad. You know I love you girl stop acting like that." I was still laughing.

"Whatever hoe. To the mall we go!" Mya said doing the Superman stance in her seat.

I loved being with her crazy ass. We made it across town to the mall in no time only because Mya was behind the wheel. It seemed like everybody wanted to be at the mall today.

"So what stores do you want to go into while we're here?" I asked because I'm not down with aimlessly walking around the mall.

"Well I want to look at some baby stores and I just want a few new comfy boots and some jeans."

She was talking, but something to my far right caught my eyes.

"Wait. Mya look over there."

"Where?"

"Over there by that black Ford truck."

"I don't see what you're talking about Alecia. That food must got you sleepy girl. Let's hurry up and go in here so I can take you back home and you can get a cat nap in." Mya said getting out of her truck.

I swear my eyes aren't playing tricks on me. I see three girls that resembled Ja'Nia, Eve, and Bianca. How is that possible though? None of them run in the same circles even though Nia and Bianca cousins, but I know since I was beefing with them, Ja'Nia was too. Last time I heard that she disappeared off the face of the earth so what the hell is she doing back in town? So many questions unanswered, but then again I could have the itis from the food I ate. I'll just push this into the back of my mind for now and enjoy this little shopping time for now, but trust me I will figure out what the fuck is going on around here pretty soon.

CHAPTER 13

Mya

Shit! I really just sat there and lied to Alecia like everything was all good. I do admit that I was falling in love with Kane, but I was also falling for Sage too. Kane has been going out of town lately leaving me alone at the house and I just feel like he's not giving me the quality time we're supposed to be having. Only reason why I really haven't told Kane yet is because I just want to make sure I know whose baby it is first. Of course if the months don't match up to the night that I had sex with Sage and the next morning after that I had sex with Kane then everything should be all good. I'll break the news to Sage first so then we won't have anything to worry about even though I know he wants this to be his child. Why in the fuck did I get myself into this situation?

I just pray that Kane doesn't find out and then try to go after Sage. I would really be heartbroken. I'm not trying to turn family against each other. I don't know why I decided not to come clean with Alecia and I had a feeling that this would come back and bite me in the ass. Why in the fuck did I get myself into this situation?

***

Alecia

I swear Mya wore me out in the mall and we didn't even go to that many stores. She was the one pregnant, yet my feet were swollen. She started to pout when I told her that I was ready to go, but when she realized when had been in the mall for almost 5 hours she agreed that it was time to go. I love my best friend, but next time I have to drive my own car so I can just leave instead of waiting on her ass.
"Bye bestie. I'm glad we spent some time together today."

"Yassssss bitch I missed you! We have to at least have an outing every week," Mya said loudly.

"Damn calm down trick and watch that bitch word. You're like my sister, but you know I don't play with that."

"My bad cry baby." Mya started laughing. "I'll call or text you later on this week about the appointment. Love you boo and tell King I said hey."

"I got you mami. I love you too and okay." I said getting out of the car and running into my apartment because it was cold as a brick outside. Locking the door behind me, I turned around the see white rose petals and candles lit literally everywhere around my apartment. It was so beautiful just like a Christmas tree. Sitting on my couch with just his basketball shorts on, I see Malachi's dick print staring directly at me. I feel like tonight is going to be the night I lose my virginity.

"Baby, what is this for?"

"From the first day I saw you I just knew I had to have you. I just wanted tonight to be special ma. Tonight is your night and whatever you want to happen will happen tonight. So tell me what your fantasy is?"

Damn. I thought to myself. *He went from "I love you and I'll protect you ma to I got stamina and I want to fuck the soul out of you tonight.* I couldn't help, but to bite my lips and stare at him.

"What's my fantasy? For you to make love to me tonight or is that too romantic for you?" I said smirking.

"Ma when I'm with you I'm Malachi, but to everybody else I'm King. You're special. So like I told you one time before ... you can have whatever you like."

Next thing I know he took my hand and lead me to the bathroom. *I'm about to lose my virginity in my fucking bathroom? This nigga better not.* I thought to myself, but I was wrong. It was a nice, warm bubble bath waiting for my chocolate skin to melt with it. He said it was for me, but I wanted my baby to join me. I wanted to feel his smooth caramel skin next to me, behind me, and inside of me. I did a slow strip to him with the song "I'm In Love With A Stripper" by T-Pain playing in my head. He was just leaning against the counter cheesing like a big ass kid. After I was butter ball ass naked I slid into the tub and made a 'come here' motion with my index finger. He stripped out of his basketball shorts and joined me wrapping his arms around my body and kissing me on the cheek.

"Baby..." he whispered in my ear.

"Yeah?"

"Are you sure that you're ready ma? I don't want to rush y—"

"Yes I'm ready Malachi. Matter of fact I'm ready right at this moment. I want you to make love to me and then fuck me until my legs shake uncontrollably." I said as I turned around and looked him dead in the eyes. He knew that I was serious so at that point there were nomore words spoken.

After we both dried off, he picked me up, and carried me to the bed. Sucking on my skin so sweetly, he made sure to leave love marks on my collarbone. He gently laid me on the bed and we shared the most passionate kiss and it got so heated that I had to break away for a few seconds.

"Damn ma, you can't take the heat? I haven't did anything major yet", he chuckled.

I rolled my eyes and said," Hush I had to catch my breath for a minute."

We both busted out laughing, but I couldn't help myself. I bit his bottom lip and sucked on it slowly. You know the sexiest thing a man can do? Well paying a bill is one, but a moan slipped out his and that turned me on to the max. I flipped us over and got on top. I admired his facial structure and kissed along his jawbone. Making sure I leave some love marks on his neck and chest I was making my way down so I could be face to face with his dick, but he pulled me back up quickly and I looked at him confused.

"This night isn't for me, it's for you. Let me take care of you ma." I simply nodded my head.

We flipped over again and now he was in control. Without warning he started French kissing my sweet spot. All you could hear throughout the room is slurping. My juices were spilling out of me like a waterfall and he made sure that he didn't miss one drop. I don't know how many orgasms I had back to back, but he indeed did have my legs shaking like I asked him to do.

"King, baby stop. I can't take anymore. Let me catch my breath please baby."

I came again. He didn't still didn't let up and I swear that I was about to pass out any minute now. As he started making his way back up my body, I braced myself for what was coming up next. I started thinking to myself *"Shit I'm satisfied from the head and I forgot the dick was coming next. Well baby girl you're not about to be a virgin anymore."* He grabbed a condom from the nightstand. I watched as he unwrapped the gold package and rolled the latex onto the head of his third leg and down the shaft. He was working with a monster! That made my nerves bad, but I was feenin' for him. Just like Jodeci said, "I can't leave you alone, you got me feenin'." It was now or never and I was ready.

When he started to put the tip in I winced a little, but encouraged him to keep going. To keep me distracted from the pain he gave little pecks here and there while giving my kitty little strokes so he could work his way inside. It hurt like hell and I mean period cramps times ten, but that pain only lasted for a minute. Soon after I felt pleasure and started moaning. Shit if I knew that sex was this good then I would've did it a long time ago.

"Mmmm shit … go deeper baby!"

"Your wish is my command ma."

He put my legs over his shoulders and lifted my body up just so he really could go deeper. He definitely granted my wish yet again and when my legs started shaking I went into pure bliss. I left passion marks on his back and he didn't mind at all.

"Oh shit I'm cumin' … I love you so much baby! Cum with me please!"

"I gotcha ma, I'm cumin' with you."

We rode the wave out and had to catch our breath. He was still inside of me and I didn't care because it felt right. He was at home and I knew at this point that I didn't want him to leave.

"You make me so happy Malachi. I don't want you to ever leave me."

"It's my job to make you happy and to protect you. Don't start talking crazy baby girl. I don't plan to go anywhere anytime soon."

"I just don't want to be left alone again."

"I told you I got you forever and I meant that shit ma. You don't have to worry about any of that."

"So when are you going to leave the streets? I worry wondering if I'll ever get a phone call saying you're dead or in jail."

"Look ... I'm not getting out the game any time soon, but I'll get out when I get enough money so we can live comfortably and without any worries."

"I hear ya King."

"Damn so you just gonna call a nigga by his street name like that? You mad at me ma?"

"No."

"Yeah you are. Give me a kiss if you ain't mad."

"Nah you good."

"See look at me you lying ma you are mad." He chuckled. "It's all good though because you still mine."

I started laughing and gave him a juicy kiss," you happy now punk?"

"Yeah I'm good."

We both started to fall asleep, but then I heard him say," I love you too ma. You got my soul."

I opened my eyes and looked at him. I just kissed him with the rest of the energy that I had and together we drifted off into the most peaceful sleep I ever had with him still laying between my legs and I couldn't have been more satisfied.

Ja'Nia

"Damn Nia is there anything else you want me to do to this nigga." Rick said.

"What do you mean is there anything else I want you to do?" I said smartly.

"I'm guessing you don't want this nigga to have an open casket funeral by any chance?" Rick asked.

"Shut the fuck up and just do what I say. You said you would help me right? What's so bad about making this look like a robbery gone wrong?" I swear my cousin was getting on my fucking nerves asking all these questions.

"Nothing you good." Rick said.

"And make sure you don't leave anything behind or this shit is going to come back ten times worst on us. We have to go about this in a smart way." I was making a plan in my head on how I was going to handle this if there was a fuck up.

You should've thought about that shit before you came in and drugged this nigga. Rick said to himself. He continued to make it look like Sage was in the middle of getting robbed, something went wrong, and his life was taken. After Rick was done and Nia was satisfied with how everything looked they left the house and never looked back. Boy, didn't they have something in store for them.

CHAPTER 14

Alecia

King's phone was ringing nonstop on the nightstand and he tried to ignore it, but it wouldn't stop ringing. Answering his phone groggily without looking at the caller I.D. and waited for the other person to respond. He didn't hear anything on the other line so he decided to say something again.

"Speak."

"Yo King we got a big problem." Kane said.

"Wassup, why you hitting my line this late?"

"Man I got some bad news my G." King heard the sadness in Kane's voice and urged him to tell him what was up.

"Go ahead and let me know what it is."

"Sage is dead man." Kane said flat out.

"Run that by me again." King said making sure he heard him correctly.

"King... Sage is dead."

"WHAT THE FUCK DO YOU MEAN HE'S DEAD?!!" King yelled.

I jumped out of my sleep. Why was this nigga yelling and it's early as hell in the morning. I raced over to where he was by the window.

"Baby what's wrong?"

He ignored me, but continued to talk to whoever was on his line.

"Aye round all the soldiers up and I'll be at the spot in 30 minutes. I should be the last one to show up and nobody better be late." He hung up the phone and finally looked at me.

For the first time since we been together King was crying. I have never seen him like this.

"What's wrong Malachi? What happened? Baby please talk to me." I pleaded.

He still wasn't talking to me. He continued to look out of the window and cry.

"Sage... Sage is dead Alecia. Somebody murked my little brother man!"

"Oh my god! What?" I was so shocked. Sage is dead?

"My fucking baby brother is dead!" He punched the wall.

"No baby please calm down... everything is going to be okay." As much as I wanted to cry I had to hold it together for my man, he needed me now more than ever.

"Nah this shit ain't gonna be okay! Who would do this shit? He ain't been fucking with anybody. I just don't understand man. I was supposed to protect him from this shit. What am I going to tell my mom and sister?" He spat out as he broke all the way down.

At this point I was holding him because he was crying and shaking too hard. My heart was hurting to see my man like this and I know that after he gets himself together he's about to go and handle business.

"Alecia I'm about to leave out for a few hours."

"King don't do anything stupid." I said to him looking him straight in the eyes.

"Don't wait up for me. If I'm still not here when you get up call me so you won't be too worried. I love you ma." He said kissing me on the forehead.

"I love you too Mali! Please be careful."

Shit! How can a wonderful night like this turn into such tragedy? Who the fuck would kill Sage. Somebody must wanted to start a war, but I know they're fucking with the wrong person. I pray that my man makes it back to me safely.

King

"EVERYBODY IN THIS MUTHAFUCKA LINE UP!" my workers scurried into place. Yeah I had the muthafucking power in this bitch.

Kane, Sage, and I have been running half of New York since I could remember and we've never had this much bullshit to deal with until now. Somebody killed my brother and until I find who the fuck it was muthafuckas were about to die.

"Who was on duty to be outside my brother's house just for safety purposes?" I said looking each one of my soldiers in their eyes. Everybody was silent and then one of them started to fidget so I assumed it was him.

"Was it you youngin'?" I asked him. He had to at least be 16.

"Yes-sss-ssss yes sir I was supposed to be on duty."

"So what the fuck happened? When I give you a task that means that you must do it correct?"

"Yes sir" he whispered.

"I can't fucking hear you!"

"YES SIR!" he said with a little more bass in his voice and poked his chest out.

"Aight so since you know that you fucked you know what's about to happen next right?" He nodded.

Without saying anything else to him I put a hollow point right through the middle of his head ending his life quickly. He didn't even get to enjoy life yet, but if you get in the game and you're not the head of the operation the only way out other than jail was death. If you live by the code then you'll die by the code.

"Somebody clean this shit up." I said to nobody in particular. "I got 5 g's to anybody who bring me some information back about my brother's death. 10 g's if you find the person who did it and bring them back to me alive got it?"

"YES SIR!" All of my soldiers said in unison and went right to work.

"Aye, Kane let me holla at you for a minute in my office." I said to him not waiting for a response.

Sitting down at my desk I waited until Kane got into my office and sat directly across from me.

"Yo King we gotta find out who did this shit man. Somebody know something and you know I got your back through whatever fam."

I heard everything my cousin was saying to me, but there was only one thing I could think about at the moment.

"Aye what happened to you linking up with Sage earlier?" staring him dead in the eyes.

"Damn you questioning me now?" Kane said grilling me.

"Just answer the question."

"Something else popped up and we didn't link up. I went out of town and I told 'em I would come through tomorrow. That's my word."

"Word is bond. Let's figure out who's after us... it can't be the Columbians cause we pay them muthafuckas on time for our shit so it gotta be somebody in the streets."

"Do you think it's an inside job?" Kane said.

"Maybe, maybe not. I'm tired of sitting on my ass man it's time to get out in the streets and give these muthafuckas a reminder that I'm the boss!" I yelled.

"Aight then I'm ready, you know I'm down for whatever."

Alecia

Why the fuck this nigga not answering his phone? It's 12 in the afternoon and he's still nowhere in sight. I thought to myself. He never did this before. I looked down feeling my phone vibrate and it was Mya calling me.

"Hello."

"Alec--- Alecia ..." Mya said sniffling.

"Are you okay? What's wrong mami why are you crying?"

"You heard about Sage right?" Mya said with concern in her voice.

"Yes I did and ever since then King hasn't been home and he won't answer his phone. Have you heard from Kane?" I asked and that's when she started crying harder.

"Mya?!"

She was still crying and didn't give me a response.

"Mya I'm about to come over there so don't leave the house."

Without letting her say a word I hung up the phone and ran to my room to grab my keys, coat, and shoes. I was careful not to drive too fast because the roads were icy. I made it to her place ten minutes flat and banged on the door.

"Mya open up the door!"

She opened the door letting me in and led me to the living room.

"Now tell me what is wrong Mya because I can tell it's more than just Sage being killed. It's something you're not telling me."

Mya took a deep breath and said," I seen Sage before he got murdered Alecia."

"What do you mean you seen him before he got killed?"

"Exactly what I said. I seen him before he died. I went over to his house last night."

"WHAT THE FUCK MYA! WHY WERE YOU OVER THERE?"

"ALECIA STOP YELLING AT ME!"

"Then stop beating around the bush and tell me what the fuck is going on."

"The reason why I was over his house is because I was letting him know that I was pregnant and to let him know that... that it might be his baby."

Wait what in the entire fuck did this bitch just say. I really had to take a moment and think about life right now.

"Mya." I paused for a second. "When did you sleep with him?"

"Look we were both drunk and---"

"Fuck all of that! When did you sleep with him?"

"It was at the party before Labor Day. Both Sage and I were drunk and it just happened. Of course we felt guilty, but just decided to keep it a secret. We didn't have feelings for each other or anything because he knew that I was in love with Kane and he was falling for Nia before she fucked up."

"What the f---"

"Wait Alecia there's more. When I seen him last night I just planned on telling him and leaving, but I ended up having sex with him again and I told him that I loved him." Mya said looking down at her hands and then a few more tears fell down her face.

"So let me get this straight," I started to say," So you fucked him and he might be the father, but now we'll never know because he's dead. Then on top of that you beat Nia's ass for trying to fuck your man, but you 'accidentally' fucked hers the first time and then turn back around and fucked him again. You fucked up completely yo. Were you even thinking about Kane once the whole time that you were out there making dumb ass decisions?"

I started to get my shit and leave. I couldn't take this. What the fuck was she thinking? I mean yeah she is my best friend, but that's some foul shit. I could never fuck somebody and their brother or cousin. I love her, but I need a break from her right now. Let me call my baby and see if he'll answer the phone this time. I hope he's okay.

CHAPTER 15

Ja'Nia

"Yeah ma," King moaned, "suck my dick just like that."

I was sitting here watching Bianca give King some mind blowing head. She damn sure wasn't better than me though because I remember right before I killed that nigga Sage I gave him so toe curling, deep throating, imma wife her type of head. Watching them did turn me on and as tempted as I was to come out of the closet and fuck King myself I had to focus and snap these pictures just so I could send them to this bitch. Let's not forget about little Ms. Mya either because Kane would be getting a nice little envelope too.

How we bumped into King was pure luck. Of course we weren't all together, but Bianca put on her game face and got his ass right where we wanted him. Yeah he was sloppy drunk and I know he might be heart broken right now since his brother is dead and I would love to console him, but right now I need his so called happy home to be broken and I won't stop until he is mine. Now here I am in Bianca's closet doing crazy shit all because he picked Alecia over me.

"Bitch get off me!" I heard King yell snapping me out of my thoughts.

"Get out of my muthafucking apartment stupid ass nigga. You can't handle me anyways!" Bianca said.

I stayed in the closet a few minutes longer just to make sure he left and then I came out.

"What happened Bianca?" I asked.

"I was giving him my A1 head and this nigga just pushed me off of him all of sudden. It doesn't matter though... did you get the pictures?"

"Bitch did I get the pictures? Hell yeah I got 'em and by tomorrow the little happy homes will be broken and we'll be one stop closer to killing this bitch."

"Cool." Bianca said as she started to look around so I just had to ask her if there was something on her mind.

"Nah... well I mean yeah something is on my mind. Have you heard from Eve today?" she asked me.

No. I thought to myself. "Nah but I'll hit her up and if you make it to her before I do call me."

"Alright will do." It was more awkward silence.

"Well I'm about to go print these pictures out and send these precious babies off."

It was starting to get awkward talking to Bianca because I feel like she was actually trying to have a friendship with me. Like ever since we were little we've never had a friendship because she just had to go around being a hoe and fucking everybody's man. One day I caught her giving my ex-boyfriend head in the bathroom at school and I beat her ass so bad that I knocked one of her teeth out in the back of her mouth. I can't think about that right now though. Time to fuck some shit up and finally get my man.

Alecia

I heard a knock on the front door and King still wasn't home. He wasn't answering his phone and Kane wasn't answering his phone either. "Call me if I don't come home so you don't have to worry." I mocked him because I feel like if you're not going to answer the phone then don't tell me some shit like that. I opened the door and on the mat was a big tan envelope. I peeked outside the door just so I could see who could've accidentally dropped it. I didn't see anybody outside which was odd, but I closed the door and sat on the couch. Once I flipped the envelope over it read, "I know this is a late present, but Happy Belated Birthday BITCH!" I just knew somebody had to be fucking with me, but I opened it anyways just to see what could be inside...

***

It was five at night and this bitch ass nigga finally came home. Shit I don't know why he came because in a couple of minutes he won't be in a fucking home. Why does he want to come in like everything just so fucking sweet?

"Baby girl where you at? I gotta tell you something ma." King yelled.

"I'm in the kitchen. I cooked dinner."

As he walked into the kitchen I was fixing our plates and I urged him to sit down.

"Go ahead and have a sit baby. I know you have had a long night and you need some food in your stomach."

"I appreciate this Alecia, but we really need to talk right now."

"Okay I hear you Malachi. We can talk while we eat dinner."

After I placed our food on the table I sat down, said grace, and started to eat my food. I cooked loaded baked potatoes, asparagus, and steaks with A1 sauce on the side. He looked at me like I was crazy because of how calm I was seeing that I haven't heard from him all fucking day.

"So you said we needed to talk so talk." I said looking at him.

"Look... I fucked up today."

"What do you mean you fucked up today? That can mean so many things so go ahead and tell me how exactly you fucked up."

"I cheated on you." He said bluntly.

"You cheated on me?" I repeated calmly. "With who?"

"It was this girl named Bianca, but look baby I didn't mean for any of this to happen. I got sloppy drunk and the shit just happened. I just got some head though and I know it's still bad, but I stopped her before it could go any further and—"

"Shut the fuck up," I said cutting him off," I know about you cheating on me. The only reason I know is because somebody left these damn pictures on my doorstop!" I threw the pictures at him. "It doesn't look like you wanted her to stop, but oh you ended up being in her bed knowing you should've been here in mine! I know your brother just got killed, but you was supposed to be handling business and then coming back home. You're a grown man though and I can't control what you do, but from this point on I am not your girlfriend. I will help you out with your brothers' funeral and then after that I'm out of your life because I can't be with somebody that cheats on me." I said in one breath.

At the moment I did see his heart break, but he fucked up and now he had consequences to pay. I loved him, but I wasn't stupid enough to stay in a relationship with him knowing he let some bitch suck his dick. Especially that bitch being Bianca. I'm tired of that bitch. She wants my life so bad, but one day she's going to get hers.

"You can still stay here, but sleep in the guestroom or if you can't keep your ass in there then just go back to your place because you're not welcomed in my bed."

"Wait hold on. I'm not going to let you leave me."

"Ha, you're not going to let me leave you? It's too late I'm already gone."

I got up and sat my plate in the sink. Love will make you do some crazy shit, but to me cheating is a choice not a mistake. He just lost me and I don't know if it's for forever, but it's for right now.

Mya

"Mya where the fuck you at?!" Kane yelled.

"I'm upstairs in the room baby... why are you yelling?" I asked.

Kane jogged upstairs to the room and found me laying on the bed watching TV. I turned around and looked at him like he was crazy.

"What the fuck is this shit?" Kane yelled throwing the pictures in my face.

"Oh my god." I whispered to myself. Who in the fuck took these?

"Yeah call on God because you're gonna need him in a minute." Kane said.

It was quiet for a long time. Both one of us didn't say anything and you could feel the tension in the air. Kane was burning a hole into my head and I was just staring at the pictures.

"Mya... what were you doing with my cousin?" Kane asked.

"I can explain baby... this isn't what it looks like!" I exclaimed.

"Explain? Fuck all that explaining shit. It is exactly what it looks like. Why the fuck were you at his house? This nigga ain't got shit on but his pants and this had to be taken right before he died so you better tell me something within the next few seconds."

"Don't be mad at me Kane." I said with tears in my eyes.

"What the fuck you mean don't be mad at you? Just keep it real ma." Kane said.

"I... I can't tell you." I said looking away from him.

"Say it!"

"Kane I'm pregnant."

"Okay you're pregnant. So tell me what that has to so with Sage and why you was over his place last night."

"Promise me that you won't hate me Kane."

"Go ahead Mya stop dragging shit out."

"It's a possibility that he might be the father." I whispered.

"WHAT THE FUCK DID YOU SAY?"

"I said he might be the father of my child!"

Without even thinking Kane slapped me so hard that he left a hand print on my face. He vowed that he would never hit a woman and at this moment I knew that he lied to me.

"What the fuck Kane! You fucking hit me! This could possibly be your child in my belly and you hit me!" I was balling my eyes out at this point.

"Shit! I didn't mean to hit you, but you just sat here and told me that you fucked my cousin and that you could be pregnant by him. I gotta go I got some shit I need to think about." Kane grabbed his coat and keys leaving out of the room and slamming the door leaving me bawling my eyes out.

I begin to talk aloud to myself. "I fucked up. I really fucked up. I can't believe this shit is happening right now. Sage got killed, my best friend isn't talking to me, and now Kane doesn't want anything to do with me. What the fuck am I going to do and I'm carrying this child in my belly? I never meant for anything of this to happen." After I said that I cried myself to sleep. I prayed that better days would soon come my way and until then I would just have to figure some shit out.

CHAPTER 16

Alecia

I refused to sit in the house and be sad over a nigga that played me. Yeah, he took my virginity and all, but what's the point of me going into a depression over him? I almost forgot who the fuck I was for a minute. Today was a beautiful Tuesday and even though it was cold as fuck I wanted to go out to the mall, probably hit Starbucks up, and go shopping.

Since King wouldn't stay up out of my face I simply told him to get the fuck out of my apartment. I know I told him he could stay in the guestroom, but he was really annoying and plus he had his own place where he could lay his head at. I couldn't shower, sleep, or even piss in peace without him trying to apologize to me. "Baby I'm sorry. Baby I love you. Baby I never meant to hurt you." I was so sick and tired of hearing the word baby it makes me not even want to have children anymore. He even tried as far as coming into the kitchen while I was cooking and hug me from behind trying to whisper sweet things into my ear. I never in life moved so fast and told him to get out of my space. That was the last straw for me and he had to go.

After getting out of the shower I applied lotion all over my body and slipped on my matching black bra and panty set. I know they usually say when a girls bra and panties match then she's trying to get some dick, but in my case I just wanted to be cute. I decided to put on a black Adidas track suit with white stripes and some white Adidas all-star sneakers with black stripes. I also pulled out my Adidas bomber jacket, black gloves, and a black scarf because it was cold as hell today. My hair was left in its natural state and I applied clear lip gloss to my lips just so they wouldn't be chapped from the cold air.

Hmm, where will I be heading first today? I think I'll settle for the mall and just get my Starbucks while I'm in there. I hopped in my car and drove to the mall in silence. I just thought how much of my life is in shambles, but now it's time for me to get it back in order. *When I get back home from shopping I'll look up some ways to invest in a business or something* I thought to myself. Driving around the parking lot for about 10 minutes I finally found a parking and it just so happen to be by the door so I wouldn't have to struggle with a lot of bags.

After I literally shopped my ass off I became hungry so of course I had to stop by the food court. Since I haven't had Chinese food in a minute I got some orange chicken, fried rice, and an eggroll with a Sprite on the side. I started digging into my food until I heard a deep voice say "Excuse me ma." I ignored whoever it was never looking up from my food and then I heard the voice again.

"Excuse me ma?" the deep voice said.

"Yes excuse you because I'm trying to eat and y---"I looked up and it was that brown skin cutie from the club that resembled Nas. Shit he was fine!

"I'm sorry for being rude. I thought it was some dude trying to talk to me and I didn't feel like being bothered." I said.

"Oh my fault then, I didn't mean to disturb you beautiful. I'll get out of your way." He said as he started to walk away.

"No!" I said a little too anxiously. "You weren't bothering me. I remember your face from somewhere."

"Yeah, we danced together at the club a couple of months ago. " He said.

I acted like I had to think about what he was talking about and then I said," oh yeah I remember now."

He smiled and then said, "Yeah ma your face isn't hard to forget. You're boyfriend isn't around is he?"

"I don't have a boyfriend." I simply said.

"Oh is that right?" He asked I guess to make sure I really didn't.

"Yes." I said giggling. "My name is Alecia by the way."

"My name is Derek, but everybody calls me Naz. It's good to finally put a name to that pretty face I've been thinking about."

He's tall, milk chocolate, and sweet too? I couldn't help but to blush.

"You're too sweet and that's funny that people call you Naz because you do look like him."

"Yeah I get that a lot. My mom was just really obsessed with Nasir and decided to make it a part of my name, but instead of it being spelled with an 's' it's spelled with a 'z'. I don't want to beat around the bush though shawty, I wanna get to know you." He said licking his bottom lip.

"Thanks for being real because I want to get to know you too." I could tell that he was shocked by my response.

"Bet so can I get your number? I would stay and continue to talk to ya, but I got some business to handle."

"Yeah, it's no problem. I'll just talk to you another time and it was great running into you." I said as I winked at him. He smiled showing his pretty white and winked walking back from the way that he came.

I wonder what his intentions are, but the vibe felt good. I told y'all miss one, "next 15" one is coming. Never dwell on a man. If he can't treat you right then I bet you that another one will treat you even better.

***

One week had passed by and today it was Sage's funeral. I helped with all of the funeral arrangements just like I promised I would and every day for the past week King has been trying to get me back, but I don't want his ass. I don't know how many times I have to say that and I wonder why he's trying to get me back now, but his dick was just down some other bitch throat and right before that it was in my pussy. One thing about today though is that it's not about me or him, it's about remembering Sage and all the good memories we had of him. Together with the family we decided that his casket would be all white with gold trim. He was also decked out in an all-white suit with a gold tie and a gold 10k ring on his pinky finger. He looked so peaceful.

Outside of the church there were security guards just in case muthafuckas wanted to do some stupid shit and let it rain today. On the inside of the church I was just praying nothing went wrong today. Once again I spoke way too soon. I was sitting next to King's mom and sister when all of a sudden there was a spray of bullets being heard outside of the church. Everybody dropped to the ground and I just prayed at that moment nobody got hurt. After a few seconds went by the shooting had stopped.

"Are you okay Ms. Ebony?" I asked King's mom.

"Yes baby, but please go and check on my son. I can't lose him when I just lost the other one." She said.

"Yes ma'am."

I got up off the floor looking around for King. *That nigga was just here a few seconds ago.* I thought to myself. Then I noticed that both he and Kane weren't in the church. I raced outside and there they were standing in front of the church. Looking around all the security guards seemed to be fine, but on the ground lifeless was my best friend Mya.

"NOOOOOOOOOOOOOO! NOOOOOO! What was she doing out here?" I cried deeply.

I ran over to where her body was laying and right before I could touch her skin King grabbed me and held onto me with all of his might.

"NO! GET THE FUCK OFF ME! WHY MY BEST FRIEND? WHY?"

While I was crying into King's chest I just happen to see Kane cradling her in his arms.

"I'm sorry. I'm so sorry. I love you please don't leave me ma." He kept whispering to himself.

"This is y'all fault! This lifestyle is killing the people we love around us don't you see this shit? Y'all should've listened when we said it was time to leave that shit alone." I yelled.

"Look baby I'm so sorry that this—"King started to say, but I cut his ass off.

"I'm not your fucking baby so don't call me that. You should be fucking sorry!" Hell yeah I was mad. The so called man of my dreams cheated on me the day after I gave my virginity to him and now my best friend is dead.

"WAIT!!" Kane yelled. "Somebody call 911 she still has a pulse!"

It didn't take long for police to arrive and load Mya up into the ambulance. Not wanting King or Kane in my sight I rode in the ambulance with Mya. I hope my best friend pushes through this. I know the last time we talked I walked out on her, but at this moment I wasn't going anywhere anytime soon.

***

Naz

"Goddamn Blu I told you don't hit nobody else but those niggas!" I yelled while we rode away from the scene.

Let me not forget to introduce myself. My name is Derek Nazir Parks, but everybody knows me as Naz. I do resemble the rapper, but I'm 6'2 and I'm from Atlanta. Some shit went down so I decided to come up to New York where my cousin Ace was running half of New York and said he had a spot for me as his right hand man since he couldn't trust anybody. Unfortunately he was murked about a week ago and word around the street it was that nigga King going on a revenge spree, but the problem is my cousin ain't have shit to do with his brother's death. Ace was all about peace and making money, but now that he's dead I'm taking over and getting revenge back on that punk ass nigga. I already let his ass go when he threatened me in the club. *"Don't touch her nomo or that's going to be ya life man."* Shit if he was a real nigga then he would've took my life right then and there, but it's aight. I still got my eye on shawty though and I will make her mine one day. It's not a secret.

"Shit I was just lettin' my shit rain boss." Blu said casually.

"Muthafucka did I tell you to let yo shit off today? Niggas don't fucking listen. You must want to run shit? You the boss now?" This nigga just irritated me. I like my shit to be precise now that shit about to turn into a mess.

"My bad boss." Blu said with his hands up.

"Ya and if those niggas ain't get hit you gonna regret that shit." I said. No more words were spoken and it wasn't a need for anything else to be said. All my workers knew what the deal was. Now I gotta prepare myself for this hit we're about to receive. A war has officially been started.

King

"Shit!" was all I could think while I was outside of the church. Today was supposed to be the day of my brother's funeral and his home going couldn't even be peaceful. I watched as they loaded Mya up into the ambulance and Alecia rode with her because she couldn't stand to be in my presence. *I gotta fix this shit* I thought to myself.

"Man what the fuck just happened?" Kane said breaking me out of my thoughts.

"Shit to be honest I don't know, but I know Mya is going to make it through man so you don't have any worries." I said while putting my hand on his shoulder.

"Look man I think we started a war with that shit we handled last week." Kane said.

"Aye we gonna talk about that another time. Let's just checks on moms, get my brother buried, and handle business." I said.

Walking back inside the church I searched for my mother and saw her wrapped in my sister arms bawling her eyes out.

"Mom are you good?" I said with concern in my voice.

"Son I don't like this. Why would somebody shoot up my baby funeral?" She said looking at me.

I sighed, "I don't know, but I promise you that I am going to handle it and everything is going to be okay."

"Malachi don't get hurt out here running these streets. We don't want to lose you too." My sister said.

"Please be safe out there. I can't lose you too baby boy." My mom said hugging me.

"I won't, I'll be safe. Now let's go say our final goodbyes and let me get y'all out of here. I would go crazy if something was to happen to either one of you."

We were able bury to finish burying my brother in peace and now it was time to go handle business and see who the fuck is coming after me.

* * *

It has been a few hours since the funeral and shooting so now I was sitting in my office. My mind was flooded with my thoughts and I heard a knock on the door that snapped me back into reality.

"Come in."

"Wassup my G." Kane said while walking into my office.

"Shit, you know handling business. You got word on anything?" I asked.

"I haven't got any word back on Mya yet, but some little nigga said he heard some nigga talkin' about murkin' Sage."

"Oh fr? That little nigga know who dude is?" At this point he had my full attention now.

"Yeah, but I gotta ask you sum'n about yo brother man." Kane said.

"Ask then cuz. You know I'll keep it real with ya."

"Did you know that Mya and your brother fucked?"

My whole face dropped. Did this nigga just say that Sage and Mya was fucking?

"Nigga what? Hell nah I didn't know about that shit. How did you find that shit out?" I asked.

"Shit Mya told me and when she did I fucked around and hit her ass then left her at the house. That was the last time I said anything to her before I seen her today." Kane explained.

"Damn." Was all I could say at the moment.

"That's not all man. Mya is pregnant and there is a possibility that it's your brother's."

What the fuck is going on around here I thought. "So you telling me that she fucked Sage and she fucked you at the same time now you or Sage could be the father? The fuck was she thinking FAM? This ain't a family love affair." I spat.

"Shit you asking me something I want to know and even though shawty was wrong I still love her and I think that she doesn't deserve to die."

"I feel you man. So what do you wanna do?" I asked.

Kane rubbed his chin and said, "you know I'm down for whatever and my trigga finger itchin' right now."

"Aight let's make this move then." I said as I grabbed my tool and headed for the door.

We pulled up to the little nigga that Kane was talking about earlier and he was outside on the corner talking to some of my workers.

"Aye little man c'mere." Kane said to the young gangsta.

"Oh shit! You're the famous Kane so that must be the famous King. Y'all are legends out here in hood! Wassup?" He said dapping Kane up.

"You mind hopping in the car real quick so my homie can speak to ya?"

"Nah I don't mind Wassup?" he asked again getting into the car.

"Word on the street is that you know who killed my brother. I put a price out for $5,000 if anybody had information for me. You got it?" I asked plain and simple.

"Hell yeah I got it, but before I tell you I want to let you know that I want to be down with the team." He had the most confident smile on his face. I chuckled.

"What's ya name lil man?" I asked him.

"It's Clarence Brown, but just call me C.B. for short."

"Well see C.B. I think you got some heart. What you doing out on the block this late?"

He got this serious look on his face and said, "I gotta feed my family." At that very moment I gained a lot of respect for him and I couldn't believe what I was about to say next.

"Aye Kane, you think little man can hang with us? You think he tough enough?"

"Ha, yeah man I think he can handle it." Kane said.

"You know it's a rule in the streets lil man?" I asked him.

"Yeah, once you in there's only one way out and that's death." C.B. stated.

"You understand that right? Once you in, you in this shit forever." I just wanted to make sure he really wanted to do this shit. It's dangerous for a young nigga like him. He should be in school somewhere learning instead of being out here in these streets. He simply just nodded his head telling me he was down for whatever.

"Aight so with that being said welcome to the team C.B." I said.

"Forreal?" He said as happiness spread across his face.

"Forreal unless you think you can't handle it. You still can back out if you want lil man." I said.

"Nah I can handle it." C.B. said poking his chest out. "And the information I got for you is some nigga named Rick said he put Sage to sleep."

"Thanks for that info man. I'll hit you up later and here go yo five stacks." I handed the money to him and he got out the car walking back to the corner we picked him up from.

"Doesn't that name sound familiar?" Kane asked me.

"I'm thinking man. I've heard it somewhere." I said.

"Wasn't Rick a bouncer or something at the club?"

"Yeah that's him." I confirmed.

"Wait, ain't that Nia's cousin?"

Now shit was making sense now. Last time I thought she had left town after that stunt she pulled, but I guess she was back now. Let me find out that that bitch had anything to do with my brother's death. By the time I'm done cleaning this shit up New York will be the bloodiest state in history.

CHAPTER 17

Big D

I knew one day I would have to do this, but I didn't know I would have the chance to do it so soon. How would you feel if you had to kill somebody you were married to? The same rules that are a part of the game mean the same things to me in marriage. I feel like Robin was a snake and I don't let snakes live. Yeah I was locked up, but it's until death do us part not I'm lonely and I need somebody to hold me at night. She fucked up when she was with that sorry ass nigga. Then on top of that she was letting him beat on her like she was use to that shit. I never in my life laid a hand on my wife or daughter. The last nigga that did lost his life and since she broke the code she has to die too.

I've been thinking about this for some minute now. Under these circumstances I don't feel bad about the shit I'm about to make happen within the next few weeks, but people need to realize that the real king of New York is back and I ain't scared of no fucking body. I don't trust anybody and that includes the bitch I'm fucking. I like young pussy, but there's plenty more where that came from so I'm breaking shit off with her tonight. Right now I'm about to go pay my wife a visit since this is the last time anybody from outside the jail will see her alive.

***

"Robin Walker you have a visitor." After the guard called her name I finally seen her beautiful face. I still adore my wife, but this is a dirty world we live in and sometimes you gotta do what you gotta do even if it's wrong. Just like if you live by the street code then you die by the street code. Ain't no way around it.

"Darren you're back up here so soon. It's been a couple of weeks, but I'm happy to see you." Robin said with a huge smile on her face.

"Robin I would say the same about you, but this will be the last time you will see somebody from the outside." I stated.

"What are you talking about?" She asked me with the most confused look on her face.

"Tell me something Mrs. Walker," I paused," why is it that you're still married to me, but you had the balls to go and be with another nigga?"

"Darren I was lonely and I was strug—"I cut her off.

"Fuck all of that! When we took our vows wasn't none of that you talking about in there! You gave my shit to another nigga and then you let this nigga beat on you like you was use to this shit. Ain't no telling what he did to Alecia if he even got that far." I calmly said.

"Don't you dare go there with me! All of those bitches you've cheated on me with in the past and then let's not forget what you let happen to her when she was younger. She was just a little girl Darren! A sweet innocent little girl!" Robin said as tears were streaming down her face. This was getting hard for me to do, but ain't no turning back.

"You know that wasn't my fault so don't try to throw it up in my face and you know I handled it. Don't try to make excuses for your fuck up. I ain't got shit else to say to you. Rot in your jail cell bitch." I gave her the coldest stare I could muster up and got up. As soon as I turned around I felt her hands around the back of my neck trying to choke me.

"I HATE YOU! I FUCKING HATE YOU!!" Robin screamed with tears and snot falling down her face.

Just when I thought about putting my hands on my wife for the first time the guards came and snatched her off of me before I could swing. Shit I'm going to miss her feisty ass, but I can always find another bitch to replace her.

***

King

After that information C.B. gave me Kane and I drove around New York to find this nigga Rick. He had to know that we were looking for him because he was nowhere to be found. I mean that nigga was straight ghost. We were sitting in my truck trying to figure where that nigga could possibly be. I know he wasn't on the other side of New York because that wasn't his territory, but there was a trap house he usually hangs around.

"Aye you think he at the spot with Richie and them?" Kane asked me.

"Let me hit Richie line real quick and peep game." I said while dialing the number.

Richie was one of my soldiers worked his ass off to be in charge of one of the houses. He is one of my trusted soldiers.

"Wassup boss?" He said answering the phone.

"Yo, you know who Rick is right?"

"Yeah he here right now. You need 'em?" He asked.

"Nah, don't even tell him I called. Make sure he stay there though and get my shit ready in the basement." I said.

"Aight one."

"One."

"So I guess I'm about to get my hands dirty?" Kane asked.

"Yeah my G. Let's head over to the spot."

It was about a thirty minute ride to the spot and all I could think about was Alecia. When I told her she had my soul I really did mean it, but it was a real slim chance that I would be able to get her back all because I couldn't keep my dick in my pants. Maybe this was for the best, but I'll always be there for her when she needs me, but if I can't be with her then nobody else will. Anyways we pulled up to the spot and Rick was looking like he seen a ghost.

"Wassup Rick? I've been looking for ya. I got a job that I need you do." I said.

"What's the job boss-ss-sss?" Rick asked me stuttering.

"Come inside and let me talk to you for a minute. Meet me in the basement." As soon as I said meet me in the basement this nigga tried to run, but before he could get far Kane came out of nowhere and knocked his ass out.

"Somebody can get this nigga off the ground and put him the basement." I said to my workers.

Rick just don't know how bad he fucked up and I'm going to make sure to leave his mom a little nice present of his remains on her doorstep.

We stood outside chopping it up before we made our way downstairs to handle this situation.

"Wake ya bitch ass up!" Kane yelled throwing some water on Rick.

"AHHHHH! I'm sorry! I'm sorry!" Rick said crying his eyes out.

"Shut up with all that yelling and crying before the next thing he throws on you is acid muthafucka!" He was pissing me off sounding like a little bitch.

"Somebody help me! Somebody help me!" This nigga kept yelling, but little did he know that these walls were soundproof. Nobody will be able to hear him scream for the next few hours.

"Get this nigga to shut up." I said to Kane. Kane just nodded his head and punched Rick in the jaw. I heard it crack and the next thing I heard was silence.

"So Rick now that you finally chose to shut your mouth. Why did you kill my brother?" I calmly asked. He just looked at me and didn't say anything.

"Muthafucka I know you heard me off you a question!"

"I ain't saying shit." He said with blood spilling out of his mouth.

"You ain't saying shit but you've already said enough. Running your mouth like a bitch you should've known that I was coming after you." He was really trying my patience.

"If you're going to kill me then you might as well go ahead and get it over with bitch ass nigga." Then this nigga had the nerve to spit on my shoes. As a reflex a backhanded him just like he was a bitch.

"You was gonna die anyways young nigga and soon enough ya dumb ass cousin will be up there with ya." I said looking him dead in the eyes.

"Aye Kane get the tools out. We about to have ourselves a little fun tonight." I said smiling.

About three hours went by and this nigga was barely still breathing. I took all of his fingers off and Kane took all his toes. I don't like muthafuckas that run their mouth so I cut his tongue out and Kane felt like he was biting the hands that were feeding him so he cut his hands off. Needless to say after all of that we weren't done with this nigga. He tried to speak, but it was too late for all of that.

"Anything else you wanna do to this nigga before I finish this shit?" I asked Kane.

"Yeah." Was all that Kane said before he got the 9 mm off the table and shot Rick directly in the middle of the head. "I told ya my trigger finger was itchin'."

"It's all good." *Ain't nobody gonna know who this nigga is.* I thought to myself.

I took the can of acid we kept in the basement for times like this. Without a second thought I poured the whole can of his body with no remorse. His cousin will be getting the same treatment whenever we find or run into her ass.

Robin

How could he just come in here and treat me like I was some random bitch off the street. Maybe I was wrong for moving on, but I didn't think he would be getting out of jail at all. I'm trying to figure out what was the difference between him fucking those bitches while we were together before he went to jail and me getting a boyfriend while he was in jail serving life. Matter of fact how was this nigga able to get out of jail so early? He's callin' me a snake, but he needs to take a look in the mirror.

I wouldn't be able to call Alecia to warn her about her father until tomorrow so I'll just have to put that on the back burner for now. I put my baby in danger and hopefully I'll be able to warn her before she gets hurt. I'm thinking about the reason why I'm in jail and shit I could've done to prevent it. I should've listened to Alecia when she said that she got a bad vibe from Tyrone. I know he was touching her because she would come and tell me, but I just convinced her that she was just having nightmares and she believed every word that I said. I don't deserve to live because the one job I did have I failed. I wasn't a mother to my child and I let Tyrone beat the other one out of me. Yes, I was 5 weeks pregnant and I didn't tell anybody because I honestly didn't know what I was going to do. When he seen that I was having a miscarriage he told me to clean that shit up and walked out of the apartment. I did as told and just wrapped my little baby up in some towels throwing it away like it was a piece of trash. That night I stayed in the shower until the water ran cold and cried myself to sleep. Thank God Alecia wasn't home that night to witness any of that.

Now that I know that I don't have Darren's protection anymore while I'm here means that I have to figure out new ways to protect myself. At one point I was untouchable and now anybody can touch me and that scared me a little. Trust me I wasn't going to go down without fighting and I will die trying to live and see my baby girl one more time. Knowing her father he's probably out feeding her bullshit right now. I should've came clean with her about a lot of shit a long time ago, but it might be too late.

Why did I even fall for him? When I was younger I never was into the hood niggas. I came from a good home with both parents and made all A's in school. I guess when my parents died I felt vulnerable and clung onto Darren. Even after all of the times he cheated on me I stayed with him. He even gave me a STD one time, but I didn't leave him just because I was so in love. I was stupid as hell for staying when I could've been with somebody else who would've treated me way better. He gave me a blessing though and it was my beautiful daughter Alecia. I know my time living on this earth is coming to an end so I hope she is guided in the right direction and not caught up with all this bullshit that has been going on.

"Aye Robin what are you thinking about so hard over there?" My cellmate Emily asked me. She was a white girl from California. I always wondered where she was from and my first time talking to her was the other day. She is sweet and doesn't bother anybody. You would've never guessed what she did. She came to New York to visit her dad and her little sisters. She walked in on her dad raping one sister and the other one in the corner crying so she killed him in a rage. I definitely wasn't getting on her bad side.

"I'm just thinking about my daughter. I wish I could be out there with her, but I know I won't see daylight anytime soon." I said.

"Well I know you're a little down, but it's time for us to head to the showers." Emily said while getting up from her cot.

"Aight thanks Emily… I'll be there in a couple of minutes." I didn't feel like moving yet. I was starting to get a bad feeling in my stomach.

"Walker get in here to shower or you won't be able to shower until next week!" I heard the guard yell.

"Yeah whatever." I said under my breath.

I refuse to be walking around smelling like ass and bad decisions so let me get up off this weak ass cot I thought to myself. I started to walk to the showers and thought about what I hated most about this place. The showers were so dingy and the floors were so fucking dirty. I never wanted to drop the soap in this muthafucka. I stripped out of the jumpsuit, grabbed my soap, and headed to a shower that was in the corner. I didn't like being closed in because if some shit was to pop off then I wouldn't be able to make an exit without being in the shit. Seeing that this was the only available shower then I would have to deal with it. I felt this bad feeling in the pit of my stomach again, but I brushed it off and continued to wash my body. Out of nowhere I felt this sharp object being plunged into my stomach multiple times. I tried to call for the guard, but nobody was there to even try to help me. I got fucking set up and I knew who was behind this. As I was trying to catch my breath all I could think about was Alecia. I wouldn't be able to see my baby girl again. I heard a guard call for help, but it was too late. I took my last breath right there on the shower floor.

CHAPTER 18

Alecia

For this past month while my best friend was in the hospital I've been spending time with Naz. That man catered to my every need and I haven't had one complaint yet. He would listen to me talk his ear off, run me hot baths, and he would even cook for me. A man that cooks? Yes please! From time to time I did think about King, but I was happy where I was at. We weren't moving too slow or too fast. I was in a good space and I was happy.

"What is your big head ass over here smiling about? A nigga make you happy huh?" Naz said smirking.

"Yeah you make me happy I must admit." I said blushing.

"Can't treat a diamond wrong. I got something for you though shawty." I swear his down south accent turned me on. I was trying to hold out on fucking him, but it was getting harder every day.

"Ohhhh give it to me!" I said sounding like a little kid.

This man wouldn't stop spoiling. He handed me this long baby blue box and when I opened it there was a Tiffany tennis bracelet with all of the charms on it. Do you know how much this shit cost? I could've bought me a damn house and he dropped it on this bracelet. That's what you call love. Wait, did I really say the L word? Aw shit. At least I didn't say that shit aloud, but I can admit that I love the things that he does for me. He literally treats me like a queen and anything that I ask him he keeps it real with me.

"Oh my god! It's beautiful Derek!"

"It doesn't shine a light to your beauty baby girl." He said giving me a juicy kiss on the lips.

I couldn't hold back any longer from not fucking him. I was really trying to see if I wanted to give King another chance, but maybe in another lifetime. I snapped out of my thoughts and realized he was playing Maxwell's "This Woman's Work". Call me old school, but I loved this song and I loved when it was played on one of my favorite movies Love & Basketball.

"Pray God you can cope
I stand outside
This woman's work
This woman's world
Oh it's hard on the man
Now his part is over
Now starts the craft of the father"

"I want to make it official with you Alecia. I've been feeling you for a minute ever since I danced with you at the club. I ain't never been tripping over a shawty like this. You got it all lil mama. Got a nigga expressing his feelings and shit!" Naz chuckled.

"Give me some time to think about it okay? I just don't want to get my heart broken again." I said giving him a weak smile.

"I'll give you some time and if so I'll wait forever. That's how valuable you are and trust me if you give me your heart then I won't break it." He said sincerely. I knew he meant every word he said.

"Let me take care of you Alecia."

After he said that it's like a fire went off inside of me. I wanted him so bad it's like I was feenin' for him. I was craving for him and I wanted him to satisfy my every need.

"Give me these moments
Give them back to me
Give me your little kiss
Give me your..."

I shocked myself when I kissed him first. Of course it wasn't our first time kissing, but I kissed him with some much passion. Just feeling his lips on mine made me cream on myself. I was that excited and I just knew this was going to be a long night.

He lifted me up and I naturally wrapped my legs around his waist and he carried me like I was feather. He started walking towards the bedroom, but I wanted to stop by the kitchen for a little foreplay. I told him to sit me down on the counter and directed him to get all of the stuff I wanted to use tonight. I told him to get the whip cream, chocolate syrup, honey, and strawberries. I just wanted to feed my baby and tease him. I didn't want to rush because I didn't want the night to end.

"Damn girl. What you about to do with that?" Naz asked looking like he never did this before.

"Boy you acting like you brand new to this." I giggled.

"I'm not ya average nigga. I ain't never did shit like this, you definitely the first." I was shocked, but I was actually happy. Just like he can show me some new shit, I can show him some new shit too.

"Let me teach you a little something like...take ya shirt off." I demanded.

"Your wish is my command." He granted my wish and his body looked like a sculpture. I mean a straight up masterpiece. His body wasn't that defined, but his 8 pack and v-cut mad me get wetter than I already was.

"Shit." I mumbled.

"You must like what you see?" he asked smirking at me.

Instead of answering him I just went to attacking his neck with my hungry kisses. I grabbed the honey and poured a little bit down his chest. Watching it slide down his chest I started to slowly lick and suck each spot I poured it in. Knowing he couldn't take it anymore he took control, picked me up putting me on top of the counter, and lifted my shirt off of my body without missing a beat. I already knew he was about to use the chocolate syrup because that was his favorite type of sweet. He poured it onto my chest licking my breast slowly and that drove me crazy so I started squirming trying to get out of his grasp.

"Nah, take this shit like I know you can. I ain't even did nothing yet." He said grinning. He continued to lick the syrup off and then said, "Don't move."

I didn't know what he was doing yet, but I was anxiously waiting. He started kissing and sucking my skin all the way down to my stomach and stopped when he got to the top off my mini loungin' shorts I had on. He looked up at making sure I was ready to do this and I nodded my head in reassurance giving him the green light. He slid my shorts off and I felt the cold air hit my kitty making me get even more excited. Never breaking eye contact from me he started to kiss around my thighs and without warming started to lick and suck on my clit. As he was killing my clit he inserted two fingers into my sweet honey pot and started off with a slow pace. The more I moaned the faster he feasted on my kitty and used his fingers to stroke me.

"Ahhhh shit Nazir baby I'm about to cum." I moaned out.

"Give me all your sweet juice ma." He didn't have to tell me twice because soon I released and was on an orgasmic high. That was the best head I have ever had in my entire life literally. He sucked the soul out of my body. I thought King's head was bomb, but Naz definitely bypassed him.

He started chuckling again and said, "Let me carry you to the bedroom bae. I see I already wore your little ass out." I playfully hit him on the arm, but I let him carry me because I knew that I wasn't going to make it on my own two feet. I forgot that we still had music playing and heard the song "If You" by Silk playing.

"Been checking you for so long
And I feel (feel)
Girl you should let me know what the deal
(What the deal)
Been peepin out yo vibe (vibe)..."

He stripped out the rest of his clothes and then helped me take my bra off. We were both new born ass naked and I never felt so shy in my life until this point. I was about to start covering up, but he stopped me before I could.

"What you trying to cover up for? You're beautiful baby girl. Let me show you how much I appreciate your beauty." Street niggas really did have a sweet side to them. It just took the right girl to bring it out of them. I just relaxed my body and let him take full control. We started to kiss again, but I wanted to feel him inside of me and I didn't want to beg for it. I bit his bottom lip gently and gave him a look like "you better stop playing with me before I beat ya ass". He didn't say anything, but positioned himself between my legs and slowly slid inside of me. I heard him grunt trying not to let out a moan.

"Damn ma you squeezing my shit!" He was fucking me and I started fucking him back. I just wanted to make sure he was satisfied.

"You feel so good baby, go deeper." I encouraged him. He went deeper and I tried to climb up the wall, but he pulled me back to him.

"Come back. Don't run away from me Alecia. Enjoy this shit ma." He said as he flipped me over and entered me from behind without missing a beat again. I made sure to put an arch in my back and I'm not talking about like the McDonalds sign. He started smacking my ass and going even harder.

"You gonna let me take care of you Ali?" *Smack!* "Let me take care of you ma, let me protect you. You gonna let me do that?" *Smack!* I heard him talking to me, but all I could really do is moan out in ecstasy.

"Naz I'm about to cum! I can't hold it in no longer baby."

"You better not leave me Ali." He spat.

I was about to go against his wishes, but I held out as long as I could before he grabbed my waist signaling me that I could finally let my nut go. Completely covered in sweat our bodies collapsed onto the bed. I just laid on his chest tracing his tattoo with my finger.

"Naz." I said just above a whisper.

"Wassup ma."

"I'll be your girl." I said.

"You sure? I don't want to pressure you—"

"Yes I'm sure. Just continue to keep it real with me and if you're not happy don't stay with me."

"I don't plan on leaving you. My word is bond. Any nigga would be lucky that you giving them a chance. You are *That Girl* Alecia."

I'm glad I have someone that finally appreciates what they have and not folding under pressure ruining something that's going good. I kissed him on the lips and we fell asleep still naked wrapped in each other's arms. It's Nazir and Ali against the world bitches!

Mya

Where the fuck am I at? Last thing I remember was being outside of the church talking to Kane and next thing you know all I see around me is white. It felt like I was floating, but I just didn't understand why this was happening.

"Mya." A voice said in a whisper. I turned around looking behind me, but I didn't see anybody. Shit was starting to get weird.

"Mya." The voice said and it sounded like Sage. I said a small prayer before I turned around again. Standing in front of me was indeed Sage and he was holding somebody's baby.

"Sage I thought you were dead." I said as tears begin running down my face.

"I am ma, but I'm in heaven." He said looking down at the baby.

"So does that mean that I'm dead too?" I asked with a shocked expression on my face.

"Nah you're just in a deep sleep right now. I was worried so I just wanted to come and check out on you. I'll always be here for you always remember that bae." Sage said as he kissed me on my forehead.

"I love you so much Sage why did you have to leave me?" I really wanted to know. I did love Kane, but I really did fall in love with Sage so there isn't any reason for me to hide it.

"I love you too ma. I won't ever leave you again. I'll always be in your dreams forever."

I believed him. Once Sage said something he meant it. That's what I really loved about him, but my next question went to this baby he was holding.

"Sage... whose baby are you holding?"

"I'm holding our baby Mya." He said looking up at me.

"What?" I asked in disbelief. "So I was carrying your child?"

"Yeah, you were carrying my child and he is perfect." Sage said smiling.

"It's a boy?" Wow. I was pregnant by Sage and now I knew soon enough I would be leaving both of them up here in heaven.

"Yeah and I'm going to make sure that I take care of him. Always remember that we will be watching over you."

I felt myself waking up, but I didn't want to wake up yet. I wanted to spend more time with Sage and I wanted to see my baby boy's face. When I finally got close enough I could tell that he was perfect. He looked exactly like his father. I couldn't do anything, but cry tears of joy. I really wish that I didn't have to go, but as I gave Sage one last kiss my eyes began to slowly open and all I could see were bright lights over me.

"Where am I?" I said barely above a whisper.

"NURSE!! NURSE!! She's awake! She's finally awake!" I heard this voice say. I slowly turned my head to see my mother crying so hard that she had to catch her breath.

"Mom stop crying I'm okay." I attempted to say with a weak smile on my face. I'm so glad that no matter what my mom will always be by my side. After the nurse came and checked out everything she said that I was fine, but I needed to stay a couple of more weeks to make sure everything was healed.

"Mya there's something I have to tell you and it's not easy for me tell you this, but as your mother I have to." My mom started to say. I hated when she starts beating around the bush and never gets straight to the point.

"Ma can you please not beat around the bush and tell me already?"

"Mya you lost the baby." My mom paused. "I'm so sorry that this happened to you baby." She said as she was hugging me.

"I already know I did mom." I said.

"What do you mean you already know? What are you talking about Mya?" She asked with a concerned look on her face.

"I seen my baby in my dreams. He was so handsome, he looked just like his father. I wish you could've seen it to ma they looked so happy in my dream" I responded smiling to myself.

After I said that my mom just smiled at me and gave me another hug. I didn't need to explain anything else to her that she didn't already know. I told my mom everything from what happened with Nia, Kane, and Sage. I didn't need to hide anything from her and I wasn't about to start now. She wasn't really fucking with Kane after he put his hands on me and I didn't blame her. I didn't know what to tell him, but I'm pretty sure he wouldn't care that I lost this baby. It wasn't his anyways.

***

I was just lying in the hospital bed watching TV when I heard a knock on the door.

"Come in." I said as loud as I could. In walked Kane with a bouquet of red roses in his hand.

"How are you doing beautiful?" He asked setting my flowers done next to me and giving me a hug. He kissed me on my forehead and I was about to wipe it off because that was the last place Sage kissed me in my dream and I didn't want that feeling to fade. I didn't though because I didn't want it to seem like I was disgusted by him.

"I'm good. I'm awake so there isn't a reason for me to complain."

"I was worried that you wouldn't wake up ma. I wouldn't know what to do if I lost you." He said grabbing my hand.

"You sure that's how you really feel? Because that's not how you acted before you left the house." I wasn't about to lay here and act like I forgot about the shit. It was the perfect time to talk about it.

"I know that I fucked up by putting my hands on you. I apologize for that. I honestly don't know what was wrong with me ma. I should've handled that a different way. I just want to work pass that and build a home with you and my child." He said. He was about to put his hand on my stomach, but I pushed it away.

"I'm not pregnant anymore Kane. I lost the baby." I spat. Looking at the reaction on his face was definitely not what I was expecting. He looked like his heart was torn out of his chest and somebody stomped on it.

"I'm so sorry ma, I should've been there for you." For the first time I seen Kane cry. He cried so hard so I just held him as he released his tears on my chest. I was over the tears. It was time to move on with my life and live. Don't get me wrong though I was heartbroken to lose my child, but to know that he was in heaven made me happy and at this point I just knew that I would be able to get through anything.

Kane

To know that I could've prevented this was breaking a nigga heart literally. There was still a chance that that baby was mine. Now we would never know and I don't even know if we will be able to move on from this. Ever since Mya came into my life it's like she changed a nigga for the better. I was still out in the streets, but every chance she got she would call a nigga just to make sure I was straight. I'm trying to figure out where I fucked up at for us to be where we are now. Maybe it was because I was never home, but I had other shit I needed to handle and now it was time for me to finish the job.

I opened my eyes and woke up realizing that I feel asleep on Mya's chest. I thought she would be sleep, but she was just up staring at the wall.

"You good ma?" I asked and when she heard my voice she jumped realizing that I was up.

"I didn't know that you woke up." She giggled. "Yes I'm good I'm just waiting for sleep to find its way into my life."

"Move over so I can lay with ya." I said taking my shoes off as she scooted over making room for me in that tiny ass hospital bed.

"I love you Mya." I said kissing her forehead and falling back to sleep as quickly as I woke up.

"I love you too."

***

I left Mya asleep and decided that it was time to finish some unfinished business. If I wanted Mya and I to work then I had to break it off with Nikki. After all this time Nikki and I still kept in contact. The whole time I've been with Mya, I never cheated on her. For the last month I just needed somebody to talk to so I've been seeing Nikki more often than I was supposed to. All of those times I was out of town wasn't mostly because I was meeting with the Columbian connect, but because I was with Nikki. I will admit when we took a little break from each other I fucked Nikki and that night she ended up pregnant. So I was stressing when I found out I had two females pregnant and that quickly ended when Mya told me there was a chance it might not be mine.

They do say what goes around comes back around and I agree with that. I was going to break it off with Nikki, but I was going to be there for my child. I don't think I can let her go cause she always held a nigga down. I remember being on the corner and she would stop by to drop everybody at the trap some food off. She even served some time for a nigga. On the real I might be in love with Nikki and I don't know a street nigga that would get rid of his rider. Yeah, Mya rode for me. She didn't do half the shit Nikki did for me. Now the only differences between her and Nikki is that Nikki is the one that's still pregnant and didn't fuck my fam. I know that's some harsh shit to say, but let's be real for a minute. Who would you choose? Loyalty is everything to me and Mya broke the code. I just don't want to leave her out here knowing she's in the hospital because of some shit me and King did. I feel like that's the only reason why I'm still here. Mya's my baby though, but Nikki will forever have my heart. I think it's time for me to pay a visit to my baby girl.

I didn't let her know I was coming, but I made that drive to New Jersey. Nikki said she wanted some new scenery so I moved her out here. She wasn't just sitting on her ass spending my money, baby girl had her own. She owned a hair salon and she had a bakery too. I think that's why I fell in love with her cause her hustle matches mine. Nikki looked just like Alicia Keys, but she stood at 5'7 with natural curly hair down her back. Baby girl body was sickening with her thick thighs and long legs. She was nothing like her cousin Eve. Eve always made it seem like Nikki was a hoe, but that was far from the truth. Those two were like opposites where Eve was the hoe and Nikki was the quiet one. It took so long for her to let me take her out, but it was all worth it.

      I walked into our condo that we shared and she was in the kitchen cooking. I heard music and it sounded like KCi and Jojo *"All My Life"*. That's funny because I remember her saying that when we were younger this would be our wedding song if were to ever get married. I laughed at her back then, but at this very moment I knew that that was what I wanted. I wanted Nikki to be my wife. I just have to find a way to tell Mya without breaking her heart.

"Babe is that you?" I heard Nikki ask as she came around the corner. I couldn't do anything, but stare her because she was so beautiful.

"Are you okay? What's wrong Kane?" She came up putting my face in her hands.

"Yeah, I'm okay. Calm down before you upset my baby." I chuckled.

"About that... I have some good news bae!" She said smiling.

"Good news about the baby?" I asked and she nodded her head.

"It's not one baby... it's two of them! Baby we're having twins!" She squealed.

I couldn't do anything, but smile because I always wanted my own family and God blessed me with two children.

"I love you so much Nikki." I said while giving her a kiss.

"I love you too Kane."

"Nah like I really love you with everything in me ma. You've held me down no matter what. You've always been my rider and I never showed you that I appreciated you. If I've ever hurt you in the past I'm truly sorry." I paused for a minute and heard "All My Life" on repeat so I figured that this would be the perfect opportunity. "With that being said I wanted to know if you would be my wife Nicole Ari Smith." I got down on one knee and pulled out this 24k diamond incrusted ring. She had tears in her eyes and for a moment I thought that she would tell me no, but to my surprise she snapped back into reality and shouted yes to the top of her lungs.

"Yes Kane I will marry you! Took you long enough to finally ask me." Nikki said while laughing and wiping the tears from her eyes.

"Oh put your hand on my belly!"

"What?! Is everything alright? Are you going into labor right now?" I panicked not knowing how pregnancy goes.

"No silly! The babies are moving. They are happy that daddy is home." For the rest of the night we made love until the sunset. I was at a happy point in my life, but soon I would have to snap back into reality.

CHAPTER 19

Ja'Nia

"Okay Eve and Bianca we can't fuck this up. This bitch has been alive for too long and this is our one chance to make sure her ass doesn't make it out alive." I said to them. Shit I've been putting my life in danger for these bitches lately so they should be grateful and not fuck up or I'm going to personally kill them myself.

"We hear you Nia. It's not like you've been doing everything by yourself." Eve said.

"Bitch shut the fuck up. What have you been doing the whole time while Bianca and I have been going on dummy missions and shit? Oh yeah I forgot trying to get your imaginary man back. He does not want you so tell me why you don't understand that shit." I said pointing my finger in her face.

"Get your fucking finger out of my face before I break it hoe." Eve spat.

"If I don't you ain't gonna do shit. Won't even bust a grape and you're talking about breaking my finger bitch please. I need you to go out and get your muthafucking hands dirty just like we said in the beginning. You're getting weak! That's why Alecia was able to beat your ass that day in the nail salon." I laughed.

"Y'all need to stop arguing so we can get this plan completed and go our separate ways." Bianca said.

Next thing you know Eve slapped me so hard that I stumbled a little bit. Oh now this bitch wants to grow some balls. Where the fuck were her balls at a few months ago?

"Yeah you not talking that shit now!" Eve said hype as hell.

"Ain't no need to talk shit hoe. That's your problem. I'm just surprised that you have finally grown some balls, but if you ever lay your hands on me again I will slit your throat from ear to ear and happily leave your body on your mothers door step bitch." I said with a huge smile on my face.

"This bitch is fucking crazy!" Eve said.

"You damn right I am crazy and I'll continue to be that crazy bitch until this shit is over."

"Well since y'all got that out of the way," Bianca said," it's time to finally get this bitch. Y'all ready?"

"Hell yes! As ready as I'll ever be." Eve stated.

"Always stay ready." I said. Then I thought to myself *it's time to die bitch*.

Alecia

"I'm so glad that you're awake now. How does it feel being up since you've been in a coma for a month?" I said to Mya.

"Yes, I'm just so happy to be alive. It just feels like I was sleeping."

"So... what about the baby?" I just had to ask because regardless of the situation I was still hoping that I was going to be an auntie.

Mya put her head down and said, "I lost the baby. I was just losing too much blood and there wasn't anything the doctors could do about it. Well that's what my mom told me. I'm sad, but maybe it just wasn't my time to be a mom even with the fucked up situation I put myself in."

"So what did Kane say about it?"

"Kane was sad. He was sad to the point where his shed some tears because he had a strong feeling that I was carrying his child, but you know with our situation he can't be that sad."

"So are y'all going to get back together or did y'all even officially break up?" I asked curiously.

"After he put his hands on m-"I cut her off.

"Bitch! He put his hands on you? Oh hell you're not about to get back with him. We don't give men like that a second chance!" I spat.

"But I know in the long run you're going to give King another chance so why can't I give Kane another chance?" she said with attitude.

"Look honestly we are both grown and I can't tell you what to do. Whatever you do I'm behind you 100% and I won't judge you. Since I know what you're going to do all I can do is support you just like you'll support me." I said in one breath.

"You're absolutely correct, but let's change the subject now." Mya said.
"Well on the bright side I met somebody." I said blushing just at the thought of him.
"You met somebody? Girl who? Awwww shit this girl got herself a new boy toy."
"Mya you're so silly, but you remember months ago when me and King first fell out and we went to the club. I was dancing on some guy and King snatched me off of him?"
"You talking about that guy that looks like the rapper Nas?" Mya asked.
"Yes girl that is him and it's funny because his name is Naz but with a 'z' instead of an 's'."
"Okay girl you better give me a rundown of your new man. I'm happy for you boo!"
"Thank you Mya."

      We talked for a couple of more hours laughing and I was catching her up on everything that she has been missing like the latest drama and I even told her that I was thinking about opening up a clothing store. I stayed at the hospital until she started to get sleepy and I told her I would be back tomorrow. I got on the elevator and pushed floor one so I could get to the parking garage. As I got off the elevator I thought I heard a noise, but I was sleepy so I just figured that I was trippen. I was halfway to my car when I heard something hit the ground and I looked back seeing no one other than Ja'Nia. *What the fuck is this bitch doing here?* I thought.
"Hey best friend. It's been a long time since we last seen each other! Aren't you happy to see me?" Ja'Nia said with this wicked smile on her face.
"Best friend? Happy to see you? You must've turned to drugs when you went away sweetheart?" I said smirking. This bitch was not about to get me hype.
"Ha you're still such the comedian. How is King doing? Oh never mind I was just with him so it's no need for you to give me an answer. I'll tell him you said hey though" She said.
"You just really want to be disrespectful don't you? It's okay though because I know you like my sloppy seconds sweetheart. If you think I don't know about Ant bitch I do. It was nice chatting with you, but I

have better shit to do than to be standing here talking to your pitiful ass."

"You won't be standing there for long baby girl." Nia said as she snickered.

What the fuck is she talking about? I felt like somebody was behind me so I turned around and I see Eve with some type of pole in her hands. She swung it and I ducked.

"What the fuck Eve you can't even hit the bitch with the pole!" Ja'Nia yelled.

Eve threw the pole down and said,"fuck it just fight me straight up hoe." So she squared up with me and I just swung on her hitting her in the jaw. She must've been practicing some fighting moves because she punched me dead in the eye and that threw me off a little bit. She didn't get the best of me because after she hit me that one time I started tearing her ass up.

"So y'all are just going to stand there while she beats my ass." Eve yelled.

"Oh that's just payback for you slapping me earlier bitch. Let's help this poor girl Bianca." Ja'Nia said.

Bianca is here too? I thought to myself while I was still beating Eve's ass. These bitches have definitely been plotting on me. I just knew I wasn't tripping that day outside the mall. Next thing I know Ja'Nia and Bianca pounced on me and literally started beating my ass. I felt punches being rained all over my body and the pain was getting worse so I stopped fighting all together.

"Knock this bitch out!" Ja'Nia demanded.

The next thing I felt was something heavy hitting me upside the head and I was out cold.

King

"Aye King!!!" Kane yelled running into my office. "We got a big problem!!"

We can never have a peaceful fucking day now can we? I thought before I responded.

"Wassup?!"

"Somebody got Alecia." He said.

"What?" I asked to make sure I hear him correctly.

"Somebody got Alecia man. I seen this letter taped to your windshield, but I looked around and ain't nobody out there."

"What the letter say my G."

"I'll let you read it for yourself fam." Kane said.

I opened the letter and it said:

"We got your bitch and if you don't do what we say then you'll find her body floating in the river. I want $500,000 in cash and I want you to meet us at a warehouse by yourself. If you're not by yourself then she dies and her body parts will be on your doorstep. We'll give you a call when we want you to come through. Don't make the wrong decisions King. I'll kiss Ms. Lady for you."

This whack ass letter I said to myself.

"Whoever wrote this shit damn sure ain't a professional and is this lipstick?" I asked Kane.

"Yeah that's lipstick so it must be a female or females that kidnapped her ass." Kane said.

"Shit man it might be, but I might need some extra help with this. Things been getting out of hand lately." I said rubbing my hand down my face.

"Who you thinking about hitting up?" Kane asked.

"Shit I'm thinking about calling Alecia's dad." I said.

"You sure about that? You know he ain't really feeling you right now."

"Yeah I know, but this is about his daughter so I'm sure he would want to know." I said as a matter-of-fact.

"Call him right now then." Kane challenged.

"Aight say no more."

I dialed Alecia's dad number and the first time it rung three times. The second time his phone went to voicemail. The third time is when he finally answered. I guess he really wasn't fucking with me forreal.

"Aye why the fuck to you keep calling my phone? You see I didn't answer the first two times so why keep calling like you're my bitch." Big D spat.

"Woah no need for the disrespect Big D." I said while holding my hands out in front of like he could see them through the phone.

"I can say what the fuck I want to say. You must've forgot who you were speaking to."

"Nah I know exactly who I'm speaking to, but you must've forgot that there is a new boss in town this go around. I ain't ya bitch and don't forget I can fuck yours if I wanted to." I said confidently. "Enough of this back and forth like some bitches though. I called you about your daughter."

"What about my daughter?" He asked sounding concerned.

"She got kidnapped."

"What the fuck do you mean kidnapped? How did you let this happen?" He said.

"Don't blame me for this shit. We haven't spoken for some weeks." I stated. "I was calling to see if you wanted to help me get your daughter back."

"That's my baby girl of course. No more needs to be said. I'm on my way to you now."

"Aig—"I was about to say until he hung up the phone in my face.

"He just treated you like you was his bitch." Kane said as he fell over laughing.

"Quit laughing nigga. I'm going to be the last one laughing when I murk this nigga."

"Oh so you want him to help you get HIS daughter back and then you're going to kill him?" Kane asked.

"Look it might not be now, but it'll definitely be later. He would be one less nigga I'll have to worry about. Now let's wait until this nigga get here so we can come up with a plan to get my baby back."

Don't worry baby girl I got you. I told you forever and I mean that. I thought to myself.

CHAPTER 20

Mya

"Good afternoon Ms. Mya Brown correct?" Dr. Green said checking her clipboard.

"Yes ma'am that is indeed me." I said.

"Ok, I'm just here to check up on you and I'm making sure everything is fine. How are you doing today?" she asked me.

"I'm doing very well. How are you?" I asked. I really just loved when people have manners.

"I'm fine. Thank you for asking and everything looks just fine here. If you need anything just push the button and the nurse will be in here to attend to you." She said.

"Ok, thank you."

Alecia was supposed to be here at 1 o'clock today to talk to me and it's going on 2 o'clock. If she was going to be late then she would've called by now. I called her phone like five times already and every time that I have called it has went straight to voicemail. *Let me call King to see if he has at least heard from her.* I said to myself.

"Speak." King said.

"Damn that's how you answer the phone now." I said with an attitude.

"Oh my bad Mya I didn't look at the caller I.D. Wassup you good?" King said.

"Yeah, I'm good. I was just calling to see if you heard from Alecia by any chance."

"Look... I got some bad news ma." His voice saddened.

"You got some bad news? What? Look I don't have time for the bullshit. What is it King?" I spat.

"Man Alecia got kidnapped last night." He said.

"What do you mean she got kidnapped last night? Where did she get kidnapped at?"

"She got kidnapped in the hospital parking from what it said in the letter."

"She was here with me last night. Wait, what letter?" I asked.

"Her kidnappers sent me a letter saying that they kidnapped Alecia and if I want her back then I have to bring $500,000 and meet them at some warehouse. Oh yeah by the way Kane is sending some security guards to stand outside of your room just so he can make sure nothing happens to you."

"It's always some bullshit going on. Look all I'm going to say is make sure you get my best friend back safely and whoever kidnapped her murk they ass." I said with so much venom in my voice.

"I got it Ms. ICU. You just lay there and get better." He chuckled.

"Whatever fuck boy." I laughed and hung up the phone on his ass. Lord I hope and pray that my best friend is ok. She was here for me so I'm going to make sure that I'm there for her. It's crazy that after one bad thing something else bad happened and now I'm sitting here thinking about the good? Sage is dead, Alecia's mom is in jail, I lost a best friend, a man that I love, and a child. When was life going to get better? I haven't prayed in a long time, but at this moment I decided to give it a try.

"Uhhh, hey God. I don't know if you hear me or not, but I know you can tell that I haven't did this is a while. It's just so many bad things happening in my life and it has me thinking if this is you punishing me or not. You took away the love of my life and my beautiful child. They say you'll never put too much on a person, but if anything else happens I don't know how I will handle it. I just ask you to look over my best friend Alecia and bring her home safely. She's the only person I got in my corner other than my mom. I just want to thank you for giving me another chance at life. This is another chance for me to live this life right and I will make you make you proud. Amen."

I know that wasn't the best prayer, but that's all I could give at the moment. Still being here in this hospital just gives me time to think and I know that when I make it out of here there are changes that have to be made.

Alecia

I woke up with my head banging and seeing nothing, but pitch black. Did these bitches really have the nerve to kidnap me and have me tied up to a chair? I told Mya I wasn't trippen when I seen Eve, Bianca, and Ja'Nia together outside of the mall that day. They all wanted one thing that they couldn't have and that was King. Did he have a magic dick that these broads were so obsessed with? I wonder where he was at in my time of need. Oh yeah, he disappeared into thin fucking air. I know that I was fucking with Naz now, but I swear I hate that I love him. Ever since I seen him that day on the basketball court, my life has been nothing but pure hell. Is it really this serious to go this far over a man? These bitches have to be desperate, delusional, or just flat out fucking crazy. "Wake up bitch!" Bianca yelled.

Next thing you know I felt water being poured on my head and the bag being snatched off just to look at these bitches.

"Hey best friend!" Ja'Nia said and then hunched over laughing her ass off.

"Dumb bitch." I said under my breath.

"What did you say bitch?!" Ja'Nia tried running up on me, but Bianca held her back.

"I called you a dumb bitch! You was supposed to be my best friend, but you running around plotting with these bitches. Same bitches we talked about! You flaw as fuck!"

I was mad as hell. I know we haven't talked as friends since that time at Kane's house, but what Nia did and said was foul as hell. Trying to fuck Kane knowing you fucking his cousin Sage and then said you was going to fuck my man if you had the chance? On top of that just want to let all the secrets out when we swore that we were going to take them to our graves. I can't trust a females like her at all.

She's a backstabber and deserves to be friends with these bitches I thought to myself.

"Aw is the little baby in her feelings? I don't give a fuck!" Nia said grilling me hard.

"Y'all bitches stop arguing sounding like cats and dogs. Let's go ahead and kill this bitch."

Eve came out of nowhere hiding in the shadows. This bitch had the most evil look on her face like she was really ready for me to die. "What would be y'all reason for killing me? You want King? Why do all of y'all want him so damn bad? You need to realize that if I don't die he'll still want to be with me and if I do die he won't be with any of you bitches. What? Are y'all going to share him or some?"

At this point I'm ready to just go ahead and get this over with, but shit got me thinking that I might live.

"Little Miss Thing you just think you the shit huh? But you're the one tied to a chair! Ever since you came into King's life you fucked up my chances of being his wifey and us starting a family together. King was my man first! I was about to have his first kid, but he made me get an abortion! All because he didn't want y'all relationship to be fucked up, but I was here first. You don't deserve him bitch you deserve to die and you're going to die for ruining my life!" Eve exclaimed calmly.

I looked from Eve to Bianca waiting on her explanation next. I was really buying time to see if I could try to get away from these crazy bitches, but it was three against one and I will do anything just to live.

"I only fucked with King because he was yours, but when we fucked around he probably told you he doesn't remember shit that happened and it's because I drugged him. Did you ever come to realize that your dad killed mine or are you just stuck on stupid? The reason why my mom and I struggled because your dad is a greedy muthafucka. Everything you have ever had becomes mine and I'll continue to fuck up your life as long as you're breathing bitch." Bianca said giving me the death glare.

Nia started talking next. "You know what Alecia...out of everything we've been through I always kept all of your secrets. Every. Last. One. Of. Them. I was there for you! I let you stay in my house and even let my parents shower you with attention. Oh yeah, King must didn't let you know that he came to see me before he disappeared those two weeks you didn't hear from him?"

I just know this bitch is lying. King wouldn't do that, would he?

"You're lying Ja'Nia. You just want to see me break and I won't. You can't break a bitch that's unbreakable sweetheart."

"That nigga doesn't love you Alecia! You're here and where is that nigga at? Let me tell you where he's at. Waiting for us to finish the job of killing you. You think he really wanted you? That day at the basketball court he was really looking at me, but you was too naïve to even realize that. You've been getting played! Ha! How do you feel?" Nia said with this smirk on her face.

I was so hurt. I honestly don't know if I should believe her or not because she's been a snake in the grass for a minute. Would King really do this to me? I was there for him through everything. Even when his brother got killed I was there. Nah, this can't be true. She's trying to turn me against him. We said forever and I hope he didn't break our promise.

POP! POP! POP!

RAT-AT-AT-AT!

Next thing you know Bianca's body dropped to the ground and Eve screamed.

"Alecia, baby girl where are you at?"

I knew that deep voice from anywhere...it was my father.

"Dad how did you know where to find me?" was all I could say before Eve and Nia pointed their guns at him. I just happened to see this expression on Nia's face that I couldn't recognize when she seen my father.

"I don't think that would be wise for you girls to do that. You have less than 5 minutes to put your guns down or my men will kill you before you even get a chance to pull the trigger." Big D calmly said.

"Baby! Baby!" King came jogging over to me and started to untie me from the chair," did they hurt you? Are you okay?"

He must've came with my father, but before I knew it I slapped the hell out of him and picked up Bianca's gun that dropped from her hands when she was killed.

"You played me! You fucking played me!"

"Alecia what are you talking about? I know I left one time before, but I had to go get info about who killed my brother. After that night I know I fucked up, but I never meant to hurt you."

"You got Eve pregnant and you planned all of this shit with Ja'Nia from the beginning. You never wanted me. You wanted her!" I said with tears streaming down my face.

"Baby... I admit that I did get Eve pregnant, but that was before I even took you out on our first date and before we even decided to get together I made her get an abortion and I never wanted Ja'Nia ever on my life I swear to you ma. Whatever she told you, she's lying. I do know that she got one of her cousins to kill my brother though, but I handled that. I was coming for you baby girl. I would never leave you behind. I told you forever."

"Shut up with the fucking soap operas. Bitch if I can't have him, you can't either!" Eve yelled pointing her gun at me.

With her sudden movement my dad pointed his gun at Eve, Eve had her gun on me, I pointed my gun back at Eve, King had his gun trained on Ja'Nia, and Ja'Nia had her gun on me.

"Your time is up!" my dad said calmly.

POP! POP! POP!

RAT-TA-TA-TA! RAT-TA-TA!

POP! POP! POP!

I feel like I was hit by a train. My shoulder was on fire and my head is hurting so bad! I felt somebody picking me up and putting me in the back of a car. I hear my father and King calling my name, but I just can't seem to focus on their voices right now. I just want to sleep.

"Shit they got away." I heard my dad say.

"We can't worry about that right now we gotta get Alecia to the hospital right now!" King spat.

"Stay with me Alecia! You're going to make it my little angel."

"Baby stay with me. You promised me forever!"

I tried to stay awake, but my eyes were so heavy. All I wanted was my man to be here by my side, but I didn't even know if I would live to see him again. I called out to him "Naz...Nazir" and then I was forced to take my last breath...